A Brownstone in Brooklyn

By

Julius Thompson

Table of Contents

Chapter One

Andy Michael Pilgrim flipped the tears from his face as he snapped his head across his wet pillow. The room seemed to sway, a sense of motion passing through his body as if his bed were cresting and ebbing like a boat on a stormy emotional sea. Andy sprung up from the bed, cupping his face in his hands. "How will I handle leaving?" he wondered.

Tension pushed Andy back onto the bed. Anxiety brought the walls closer. Keeping his eyes closed, he slipped deeper into his thoughts. "When I left to spend that summer in Georgia, Mamma cried." Andy rolled over in his sweat. "Now, I can't imagine how she will react."

He opened his eyes and stared at the dark window that beckoned only four steps from his bed. Andy kicked the forest-green sheets and maroon comforter off his sweat-covered body.

He felt for the remote on the night table. The light from the TV screen penetrated the darkness. What Andy saw was one of those old black and white movies. It was a scene where a young boy was leaving home for the army. The young boy felt his friend's mother horror when she read the telegram from the army telling her about the bravery of her son, and how he died defending his country. Now, the negligible chance of the young man's survival was evident in his face. The young man's face on that television screen reflected how Andy felt.

Gradually, Andy drifted back into a restless sleep. The roar of a Brooklyn City bus speeding down Gates Avenue in Bedford-Stuyvesant startled him. A young person of the sixties shouldn't be scared, he thought, but he was. He remembered sitting on the stoop in front of the Brownstone and a bullet streaking over his head. Andy had ducked. If the bullet were meant for him, ducking wouldn't have done any good. At that moment he'd ducked, but fear was still biting into his being tonight.

The television showed a lover's quarrel bringing conversation into the room. Now, the soldier and his sweetheart looked at each other and realized this could be the last time they would see each other. The soldier kissed his girlfriend and then walked out.

Andy turned off the TV and turned on the radio. The soul station, with the famous call letters WBLS-AM, was playing. The announcer said the weather was typical of late spring: hot, humid and in the nineties. What caught Andy's attention was the last thing the announcer said, "President Lyndon Johnson ordered an increase of American forces in Vietnam." Andy had thought the Vietnam War would dissolve as a fairy tale of heroism on the cover of Time Magazine. Now, it was up close and personal. Since he got the letter that required him to appear at the military draft board for his physical, he'd spent many sleepless nights worrying about his future.

Andy flipped his legs over the side of the bed. Time passed. He heard another bus gliding past his family's apartment, finally squeaking to its regular scheduled stop at Gates and Nostrand avenues.

Andy stared at the window, walked over and gazed at the four-story building at the corner, adjacent to Mr. Possum's candy store and about a half-block from his own apartment building.

In five hours he would face the military draft board. It was either finish City College of New York or board a military jet to Southeast Asia. Here's the Vietnam War with all its bitter reality.

He turned and walked to the bed and plopped down. He rolled over on his side and faced the wall. The street light shimmered, danced and made vague images on the yellowish gray wall. The hours dragged.

He swayed with the rhythm of his thoughts. "Vietnam, Vietnam, I don't want to go!" But it was time to dress and catch the subway to his appointment with the draft board.

Andy stretched, jumped up and walked to the bathroom. He switched on the light, turned on the warm water and looked into the mirror. He leaned forward and stared. His skin was a deep Milky Way chocolate and his eyes a light water-colored brown. His hair was very soft, curly and parted on the side. His lips were dark, but had a reddish tint. His look was exotic with a feel of the West Indies. Hi gaze revealed something strange. "This isn't me...my eyes, my nose and mouth are mine, but it's not me." What stared back were blood-shot eyes, caused from a lack of sleep.

He put the wash cloth into the warm water and squeezed the soap lightly. On the radio the Drifters sang "Up on the Roof." Andy knew some of the words and continued to sing as he walked back to the bedroom.

The song faded out. Andy walked over to the radio and turned the knob creating an eerie yet comforting silence. He walked to the bedroom and put on his clothes, which he'd ironed and laid neatly on the chair. He dropped four quarters and eight dimes into his pocket for his rides on the subways today.

Andy walked to his mother's bedroom. He stared at Golda, then looked at the empty spot next to her. His father, Marvs, left at 3 a.m. for his job with the Metro Yellow Cab Company.

She was tossing and turning in her sleep. Last night she'd cried and hugged him. She'd released him, crawled into her bed and sobbed.

This morning she rolled over, looked up and grabbed Andy and pulled him close. Andy kissed her on the cheek. "It's time, I don't want to go, but I'll call and tell you what happened."

Releasing her son, Golda slowly let Andy's hand go. "Andy, baby, I hope everything goes all right. I don't want to lose you to no war."

"If everything works out, I'll be able to finish City

College." He pulled his hand away and walked out of the room.

"Be careful."

Chapter Two

Six a.m.

Andy closed the metal door of his fourth-floor apartment and walked down the three flights of wooden, tile-covered stairs. He hesitated at the front door, took a deep breath, opened the door and walked onto Gates Avenue, past Mr. Possum's Candy Store, the barbershop and eventually reached Nostrand Avenue. He fast walked the six blocks to Fulton Street where the "A" train would convey him to downtown Brooklyn.

On the Nostrand Avenue subway platform, he slipped a dollar through the small u-shaped opening in the glass to the cashier. She pushed back a token.

Andy walked through the turnstile, heard the coin box click, pushed the arm and walked onto the platform. It seemed he should be riding the subway all the way to 137th Street for his classes at City College; instead he was catching the Euclid Avenue BMT subway to the draft board in Sheepshead Bay.

At the edge of the platform, Andy peered down the tunnel into the darkness, then stepped backward, to the bench, sat down and closed his eyes. "I'm afraid."

The rattling train's blaring horn sounded in the distance. "I won't get on that train."

The train's screeching wheels sent chills racing up and down Andy's back.

He yelled out loud over the trains squealing stop. "I'm not going!"

The subway pulled into the station. "Vietnam or college?"

Andy walked back toward the tollbooth, then turned and sprinted through the subway car door.

The doors closed.

Andy plopped down onto the hard gray plastic seat. Some people were reading *The New York Daily Times* and some *The Daily News*. Some wore blue sanitation uniforms and others in pinstriped business suits headed to jobs in the tall buildings of Manhattan.

Andy leaned his head back onto the large plate-glassed window. The tunnel lights were blurring and blending as the train sped though the tunnel. Just like his thoughts that rammed against each other so did the lights along the tunnel walls. The lights weren't clear, and like his thoughts, obscured.

Andy stood up, walked toward the door as the train pulled into Hoyt Street station. He turned, watched the door close, and then walked through the tunnel to the BMT station and to the train that would take him to his destiny. The 15-minute ride seemed longer. Andy got off the train and stared at the old three-story red brick office building that housed the draft board.

Chapter Three

Seven-Thirty a.m.

Andy approached the tail-end of the one of the draft lines. It seemed every eighteen-year old Brooklyn male was here, shuffling toward a military man at a desk. Each interviewer had a stack of papers and when a potential draftee approached, the military man searched for his paperwork. Before a young man walked up to the desk, the apprehensive inflections of Mong, Spanish and Brooklynese would give away a nervousness that infected the next man in line.

The rich kids from Flatbush didn't have to worry; influential people would get them a draft exemption. Andy noticed the general poor-class appearance of everyone in line. He saw fear in the faces of the young men as they inched forward. He saw his friend, Jose Morales, from Eastern District High, and an Asian fellow, Tony Yang, who he'd competed against in an Academic Bowl at Brooklyn Tech.

"I've been dreading this day," Jose said.

"You're not the only one, I haven't slept much, "Andy said, "sweated, tossed all night long."

"Same here, anyway, good luck."

"Same to you." Andy walked towards the glass doors.

"Have your letters ready," a military officer barked at the young men.

Andy handed his draft date assignment letter to the military officer with the steel-gray eyes. The man pointed to a door on the right. After looking at each letter, the potential draftees were directed left or right. The next man, sitting at a desk, looked at Andy and took his letter.

"You're in college?"

"Yes sir, I'm a senior at City College."

"Any illnesses?"

"Yes sir, I have a chronic sinus problem. I've had those

drained two or three times, the doctor thought they'd have to be operated on and sometimes it gets so bad they bleed and bleed...."

"Okay, Okay, are you an only son?"

"Yes Sir."

"Get your physical and come back to me when you're finished. Bring the results back."

Chapter Four

Eight-Thirty a.m.

Andy walked into the room with what seemed like hundreds of young men who were given paperwork to carry to every station. There were urine samples, then needles punctured arms for blood samples, and cuffs tightened for pressure readings. Doctors peered down throats. From one group of doctors to another, they went.

Ten-Thirty a.m.

Andy walked back to the first desk where the military officer was waiting. Now, he would be told the outcome. If he received an "A" rating, he'd be drafted. He handed themilitary officer the completed paperwork. The officer peered over each page. Andy swayed a little, and thought, Saigon, here I come.

The officer looked up. "Mr. Pilgrim, upon review of our records and the results of the physical exam the army has found you...4F."

Andy blinked.

"You may go."

"Thank you."

Andy turned toward the double-doors. He looked down the street for a pay phone. He sprinted toward the phone booth, then opened the door and reached for the receiver. Andy saw other young men making calls. There were cheerless faces. Andy fumbled in his pocket and found the exact change for the price of the call and dialed his home number.

"Mamma, I've been turned down! I'm 4F because of the chronic and severe sinus infections. They said it was a good possibility of that leading to something more serious, because of that they wouldn't take me into the army."

"Thank God!"

"Mamma, it's a big burden off my shoulders."

"You coming home?"

"Naw, I'm going to City College and I'll see you tonight."

Andy hung up the phone, turned and walked down Euclid Avenue to the BMT subway station. As he glanced back, the line of potential draftees was still coming out the door. Andy's sigh of relief reverberated off the old office building.

Chapter Five

Golda heard Andy's steps when he left earlier in the morning. She closed her eyes and prayed. She never stopped praying until she heard the phone ring.

After hanging up the phone with Andy, she dialed her close friend, Sister Love, who lived on the third floor.

"He's not going."

She then called the office of the Metro Yellow Cab Company and left the same message for Marvs.

Golda hung up the phone and rolled over and stared out the window. "No war for my baby."

She cried.

Chapter Six

Sister Love

From New Orleans she brought her distinctive personality to Brooklyn. Her friends called her Sister Love because she loved everything with passion. Her flavor spiced everything and everybody. She could also hate with passion. Her name was spontaneous, nobody put any thought in the name, and it just evolved. She was a passionate woman. Passion for her was love and love was her passion.

She knew every juicy incident that happened in the lives of everyone living in the four-hundred block of Gates Avenue. Some people said that as something unfolded, Sister Love was there recording every detail.

From her apartment window, which people called the "Eye That Knows All", Sister Love observed her neighbors' lives. She kept the big picture window clean so nothing could diminish her view of life on Gates Avenue.

Gates Avenue meandered through the middle of Bedford-Stuyvesant like a long strip of concrete ribbon that twisted and turned creating an avenue of change. Brownstones, separated by multiple-story reddish–toned apartment buildings bordered both sides of the street.

There were old-generation Blacks left on the Four-Hundred block, who migrated in the forties and early fifties from the deep south, but now the northern-bred sixties generation was transforming the residents' static ideas in this Brooklyn neighborhood.

The four-story Brownstone at 423 Gates Avenue was located in the block where the Civil Rights movement, gangs, and drugs were seeping into everyday existence. All these changes Sister Love noticed with a weary eye.

Sister Love reached for the window cleaning fluid. She sprayed the mist on the dirty window pane until the milky fluid formed droplets that rolled down the glass. She glanced back to see if Jon was awake.

"Get your lazy butt up and get ready to get outta here." She continued wiping the window pane.

All morning she cleaned the apartment, the windows being last. Her eyes squinted in the sun as she watched Jesse Towns walk out the door and down Gates Avenue. "Keep walking you son-of-a..." She caught herself. "Don't look back or I'll shoot you! You ain't selling this building." She hurried to catch the bus for her job at the A&S department store in downtown Brooklyn.

Sister Love walked to the kitchen and got a glass of water. She walked into the bedroom, threw the blanket off Jon and tossed the cold water in his face. "What the..." Jon leaned his body forward, half asleep, and put his bare feet on the cold wood floor.

"I said get up and outta here! If I have to work, then you'd better find some of your old cronies to be with because you ain't staying in this apartment while I have to work that A&S lunch counter." She walked back to the window and saw Towns enter the barbershop.

As a nine-year old kid Towns was called a fidget, which was considered a half a midget. At 5-2, you don't get much respect. When you looked at Towns you saw two ears sticking out from a head positioned inside a miniature frame. Now, he owned 423 and wanted to clean out the residents to make room for efficiency apartments. Towns was in deep thought.

Towns rubbed his chin and pondered. "If I can't make efficiency apartments, then I'll sell to urban renewal and get rid of the problem." It would ease his money strapped condition. If only those urban renewal people hadn't alerted the residents. "Damn, I would've been free to do what I wanted with the building. Now, those families are getting so they hate me and sometimes I don't want to go back to my basement office."

That Pilgrim boy, Andy, knew too much. "He's a smart

one. I could've sworn I heard him listening in on my conversation. Well, guess what, I'm going to make sure he doesn't do that again. I've got a few surprises for him."

The Yellow Cab's brakes squeaked, making a loud racket that brought him back to reality and caused Towns to search for the noise. He glanced over his shoulder and saw a pair of eyes staring from the second floor window. He thought, "I'd better get outta that crazy woman's sight." Towns turned and walked toward the Hair is Art Barbershop.

At the center of the block, next to Mr. Possum's Candy Store and Yang's Chinese Laundry, stood the barber shop where people talked politics, who was sleeping with whom, the latest gambling daily number and the current news from the civil rights front.

Steward's Music Exchange stood at the corner of the block where you could buy the latest hit song on a 45 record and play your illegal daily number.

The four-hundred block of Gates Avenue had everything from fast-food places to places to find the body of a person before they went to their final resting place. People lived next to the two funeral homes across the street from each other without feeling squeamish. It was as natural as living next to the fish market, Chinese laundry or the candy store.

Towns walked into the barbershop, just as James Randall turned the corner from Nostrand Avenue. Randall's light-brown eyes were in stark contrast to his dark skin that seemed to come from all the time spent working under the hot sun in the tobacco fields of southern Virginia. His skin was in contrast to the light tint of his eyes. His eyes scanned the block to see if there was anybody watching as he walked toward the apartment. A scowl was a permanent fixture on his face. He grunted to Sister Love as she came out of the building.

"Stop looking ugly." Sister Love smiled at Randall, who unlocked the door to his apartment, almost slamming the door in her face. "And a good morning to you..." She greeted him as she was walking out the door. Sister Love learned from her common-law husband Jon, who was from Richmond, Virginia, that he suspected Randall of being the prime suspect in a murder case. Two men had fought in a bar and Randall was the only one still living.

Sister Love made the walk to the bus stop for the fifteen-minute wait for the B-52 bus. She passed the barber shop and gave Towns a dirty look. He pulled the newspaper in front of his face. She knew Towns had broken some laws involving taxes. He was in trouble and trying to get money to keep the government from taking the Brownstone. If pushed, Towns knew she could make a call and get him put in jail.

Sister Love's light-brown skin and gray eyes gave her a look you found in the Creole's of New Orleans. She still had a slight Louisiana accent. Today, she sported a brown wig, one of the many from her varied collection, which included a blonde, brunette and multi-colored. She never had much natural hair, so Sister Love always wore wigs. From her teenage years she developed her wig collection. Jon teased her about her wig collection and how she had too much of other people's hair. She always yelled back, "I bought it, so it's my hair."

Sister Love leaned against the bus pole. Al Green's latest hit "How Can You Mend A Broken Heart" could be heard from the loud speakers outside Steward's Music Exchange.

She leaned forward to see if the bus was coming and got a glimpse of it about three blocks down Gates toward Broadway. Then her gaze moved to the apartment building. James was really worried about something. Anything could set him off.

Randall slid the backpack off his shoulder and onto the floor. He walked to the refrigerator, grabbed a beer, then went back to the living room and found a chair. He opened the beer and took a big gulp. The cool beer washed the grit down his throat. Cleaning the classrooms at Brooklyn Boys High all night and into the morning made him thirsty, but he knew better than to drink on the job. That was one of the reasons he'd left Virginia. At least the Richmond authorities didn't know where he was hiding. This block, in the heart of Brooklyn, was a nice resting spot. He may have to move soon, but for now this was home. Randall slid into deep thought."I hope this deal with Peter Paterson works out, and if it does, I'll have some big bucks and get out of Brooklyn."

Randall stopped smiling when he lost one tooth on the left side of his mouth, from a bar fight, and one on the right side from an encounter with his girl friend's fist. He would neverbe a smiley-faced model. He felt people were always looking at him to be critical.

If people couldn't get close to him, then he didn't have to reveal a lot about himself. Randall leaned further back in the chair, closed his eyes, but not his mind to his thoughts. Fear of discovery can make you do strange things.

Sister Love found a comfortable seat in the middle of the bus, across from the exit door. As the B-52 bus headed downtown, she leaned back and watched the various city blocks pass.

Towns waited his turn. He pulled his *New York Daily News* down from in front his face and watched as Sister Love got on the bus. He figured Randall was in his apartment and after getting his haircut, he'd get in his car and drive to Jamaica, Queens. He didn't want to stay in this area, because he thought living in Queens made him superior to these folks in Brooklyn.

Chapter Seven

The most special times in a person's life are not meant to last forever. They're like bubbles rising from a plastic ring dipped into a soapy solution. The soap bubbles rise, with the sun flashing brilliant colors, then burst into a showering memory mist.

From her bus window, Sister Love watch the little kids running in the spring breeze making bubbles rise and fall. They giggled and pranced around an imaginary pole. She watched as the bus turned the corner to the street that would take her to downtown Brooklyn.

She thought about her family, which she called her neighbors, who lived in the Brownstone. Even when she had drinking binges, she had people looking out for her. She smiled when she thought about the time she staggered up the steps and sat down in a kitchen chair, when there was a knock at the door. There stood Andy Pilgrim.

"Sister Love I found your hair on the stairs and thought you might have misplaced it." Andy kept a straight face as he handed the wig to its' rightful owner. Sister Love closed the door and let out a big brassy laugh that scared her husband. "Go back to sleep."

The bus turned the corner onto Fulton Street, with downtown Brooklyn off in the distance, bringing Sister Love back to reality. She saw the Brooklyn Fox Movie Theater and knew she was near work. She closed her eyes, just for a few seconds, and knew when she got home, she'd have a talk with Randall.

The ringing phone startled Randall and he squeezed the chair with a death grip. Randall stared at the phone, but didn't answer. He kept saying to himself, "Keep ringing, but I'm not going to answer, damn I'm out of cigarettes. Possum better have some this time." Randall grabbed his coat and walked briskly toward the door. The phone was still ringing.

He closed the door, almost knocking Golda down as she turned the corner on the steps.

"Sorry." Randall steadied Golda.

"In a Hurry?"

"Just going to Possum's for some cigarettes."

"I'm going to Long Island, Mrs. Freedman is having an afternoon brunch and I have to serve."

They walked down the steps. As they passed the barbershop, Towns was getting into the chair and quickly turned his head when he saw Golda and Randall passing the shop.

Randall stepped into Possum's candy store.

Golda kept walking. She hummed the tune from Ketty Lester's "Love Letters" that was playing over the music store's loud speakers. "I'll kiss the name that you sign and darling then I'll read love letters straight from your heart...I'll memorize every line and I'll kiss the name that you sign."

Her body swayed to the melody that had a blues feeling and reminded her of Georgia and that down home country feeling. Golda crossed the street and waited for the Nostrand Avenue bus to take her to Atlantic Avenue and the Long Island Railroad and then the ride to the Hampton's in Suffolk County.

The barbershop was a social center as well as a place to cut hair.

"Not much from the top and a lot off the sides."

Lenny moved Towns head from side-to-side to get the best angle.

"That Martin Luther King fellow is getting our community together."

"Yeah...but you know it's going to be trouble in all the Negro ghettos, especially in cities like Detroit, Los Angeles, St. Louis, Chicago, Newark, Philadelphia and even in New York, whether it's in Harlem or Bedford-Stuyvesant."

"Hell... if they want to bring it on, do it...bring it on,

people are game," someone yelled from across the room. "Look at this block, if it wasn't for this barber shop, Possum, and the music shop, we'd have nothing. And around the corner on Nostrand going toward Marcy or even the other way toward Lafayette we own nothing...you hear me, nothing."

The sound of the clippers and the voices from the television lent an interesting background to the conversation.

"All that's well and good, but what makes me mad is some people in our community are some of the biggest leaches."

Towns visibly cringed.

"They say they're for us and yet, they're like the white folks who own places on Gates Avenue, and leave for nice homes in places like St. Albans, Queens."

Towns wanted to get up and leave but couldn't since Lenny was still cutting his hair.

"I know they're talking about me."

"Relax Mr. Towns...I almost cut you."

"Sorry."

Lenny finished the stylish cut with a strong brushing and some spray cologne. Then he unhooked a button so he could remove the white cape covering Towns' clothes so he wouldn't be covered with hair. He did that with a flourish, knocking hair on the floor around the barber's chair. Towns, got out of the chair, gave the barber a good tip and exited the shop. He headed to his office in the Brownstone.

"Good...everybody's gone."

Towns climbed the flight of stairs and closed the door behind him. He called the Housing Authority and got the answer he wanted. It was time to get rid of the building.

He placed the phone back into the receiver and turned toward the cabinet. He heard the squeaking hinges on the door behind him. He turned around. Towns didn't blink. No sound came out of his mouth.

"Bang!"

Towns crumpled on the floor.

Chapter Eight

After four children, Trina Paterson maintained her shape. She was 5-4, light complected and carried herself with a quiet dignity. Male suitors called her a pretty redbone.

Today, she moved around her apartment, cleaning, making sure it wasn't a disaster. Her youngest child had left for school a couple hours earlier. Her family kept her active, especially the one who worked as a part-time bartender at the Brevort Theater on Bedford Avenue. When the "Soul Reviews" came to the neighborhood, then he found work. Other than that, he remained unemployed.

Her son, Peter, worried her the most of all her children. He was a natural athlete, but failed in school. She loved watching him pay basketball for Boys High. He was a prizefighter on the court with a boxer's mentality. People didn't realize this was part of his personality and gamesmanship. Some people didn't like him. Some people did.

He had hoop dreams. He had hope. He wanted to do something with his life. However, he wanted it quick. He wanted it fast. He wanted money. The best way to get money was to sell drugs. To get the drugs he joined neighborhood gangs. He dropped out of school. Peter changed forever. He was a drug dealer.

When he lost his dream, Peter hated anybody that was doing something with their lives. Trina was afraid for Andy's life, for she knew Peter hated him. She knew he was planning something, but she couldn't make him tell her. She prayed for Andy.

Trina worked around the house, trying to figure out what she could do. Her latest boyfriend, Fred, was on a construction job in Flatbush and might be home for lunch, so she'd better have his food ready

While washing the last of the breakfast dishes, she thought

she heard a loud noise in the basement. She wasn't heedful or scared, but she did hear somebody slam the front door.

She walked through the living room and into the children's bedroom facing Gates Avenue. The apartments were built like railroad cars where you could see from one end to the other. Someone in a green athletic jacket with a gold trim down the sleeves and legs was walking out the door. He looked up and down the street, then moved in the direction of Elm Street, opposite Nostrand. Trina walked to the kitchen and finished the breakfast dishes. She cringed.

At first Towns wasn't aware of his surroundings. When he moved, a searing pain shot through the upper right side of his body. He reached, felt something sticky on his blue shirt. Towns turned his head and saw blood dripping from the wound.

Towns leaned forward, but felt slightly dizzy. He continued until he reached his feet. He staggered to the door and used his one good side to crawl up the steps. He grabbed the railing along the wall. At the top of the steps, nearing the Paterson's apartment, Towns leaned forward and tapped on the door.

"Help me." No one answered.

He tapped louder.

Trina looked through the eye-level keyhole.

"Who is it?"

"Help me."

She opened the door with the safety latch still attached and looked down the crack between the door and the wall and saw the bloodstained Towns. Trina stepped back from the door, hesitating. She eased forward and unlatched the door and reached down to help Towns.

"Oh my God...what happened?"

"I was taking something out of the file cabinet when I turned around and saw this man. I didn't recognize him and the next thing I knew I had this stinging in my chest."

"Wait, let me call the ambulance. Stay right here!"

Towns propped himself against the hallway wall and tried to keep from slipping into unconsciousness.

"They're on the way."

Trina didn't like Towns, but she was overcome with the thought of another human being hurt. She brought a pillow and made Towns comfortable.

In a few minutes, Trina heard sirens and went downstairs to open the front door. The emergency squad came and carried Towns to Kings County hospital.

Chapter Nine

The street was alive with people hustling to neighborhood stores to finish shopping. The street buzzed with news on the Towns Shooting.

Towns was back in his home in Queens, after his visit to Kings County Hospital.

"What happened?" someone asked.

"Who knows," a customer answered.

"Somebody in that building doesn't like him and it's going to get worse...they didn't want to kill him, just send a message."

Lenny kept cutting hair.

Outside, people visited the Music Exchange or Possums' candy store. The Chinese laundry was busy as people were leaving dirty clothes and picking up freshly starched shirts and pants. There would be Cocktail Sips around Brooklyn, but a lot of people were getting dressed for the Soul Review at the Brooklyn Brevort Theater.

The teenagers were singing the lyrics from The Drifters' hit song "Up On The Rood" and The Miracles' "Please Mr. Postman." Mary Wells' "My Guy" had the younger Brooklyn crowd ready for love. Everybody was waiting for the last act at the Brevort with the melodious Al Green singing his hit "How to Mend a Broken Heart."

Early afternoon was a busy time at 423 with every apartment bustling with domestic duties and preparation for going out Saturday or spending a day at church on Sunday.

Andy was sleeping when he heard Golda on the telephone calling Trina discussing the shooting of Jesse Towns.

"Can you believe it?"

"He deserved it...but I'm glad it was only a flesh wound and he's home now," Golda said.

"Yeah...he's trying to put us all out in the street..."

"How'd they get into the basement without someone opening the front door?"

"You know as well as I do that somebody in this building is involved...I mean we'll all be suspects if something happened to him," Golda said, walking toward Andy's room with the phone, which had a long extension cord, the phone pushed hard against her ear.

"Listen I'm going to call Sweet Thang and Mother Nature to see if they've heard anything."

"Tell both of them to keep everything cool on Exeter Street."

"I will."

"...call me back and let me know if you hear anything...goodbye."

Golda hung up the phone.

"Andy...Andy."

"I'm up...why don't your friends have real names?"

"You mean Mother Nature, Sweet Thang and Sister Love?"

"Yeah."

"Well, it just makes us different."

"They call you Mamma and Poppa and I have trouble telling who's who."

"I know, ready to eat?"

"You bet."

"Big date tonight?"

"We're going to the Brevort...to watch Little Stevie Wonder, but they've got the oldie crowd..."

"I'd rather hear Linda Jones and Ketty Lester than that Marvin Gay."

"Well, Leslie and I will just have to endure those old folks until they put the real singers on stage."

"Leslie Groves?"

"Yeah, my dark-complexioned beauty with the long black hair that shines like polished coal. She's the best-looking girl at Brooklyn College. It's going to be great at the Brevort."

Chapter Ten

Andy and Leslie got off the Brooklyn City B-38 bus at Bedford and Fulton Street. They strolled down the short block to the Brevort Theater. They held hands and moved toward the long line that formed outside the theater. The late Saturday afternoon sun caused people's eyes to squint as the lights flashed on the marquee.

Brooklyn's hip crowd was in the lobby of the Brevort. The "Cool Cats" and their ladies arrived from Bedford-Stuyvesant, Flatbush, Brownsville, East New York and Bushwick. Growing up in Brooklyn meant dressing and imitating your favorite singing group.

If you were a wanna-be member of the Temptations you wore black rimmed glasses that complimented an Afro hairstyle that was so high it forced you bend at the knees to get inside the doorway. You would sing the lyrics to your favorite girl.

This crowd showed Brooklyn was the place to be in the sixties. The songs of the sound groups helped retain a spiritual center when H. Rap Brown was saying "Burn, Baby, Burn," Martin Luther King was shouting from Atlanta that "We Shall Overcome" and Malcolm X was spreading "the bullet or the ballot" in Harlem.

It was a time of the radical racial consciousness when Negroes became Blacks and processed hair was replaced with the natural Afro. After the James Brown Anthem "I'm Black and I'm Proud," people walked with their back straight. When Martin Luther King said, "Nobody can ride your back if you keep it straight," the gulf between him and Malcolm wasn't as wide.

The love ballads of The Temptations and other groups were saying that the power of the people came when two people held hands. Women were put on a pedestal and men swore they would do anything for the love of a woman.

Tonight, everybody wanted to be an icon of fancy dress and fancy steps when the after-concert parties got underway. Everybody went to parties called "Blue Lights In The Basement" because the parties were in basements of Brownstones and the ceiling lights were blue. Everybody would be ready to show off when the concert was over and the basement parties began.

Now, everybody was in a place where all outside pressures were suspended and the universe consisted of the people on the stage state and in the audience. It was a time for soul love. The walk, the style and the funk were all on display.

Andy squeezed Leslie's hand and moved closer to kiss her, ever so gently on the lips. He moved back and smiled as Lenny Welch sang, "When you give love and never get love you better let love depart...I can't get you out of my mind...you made me leave my happy home...since I fell for you."

They moved closer and held each other tighter. Throughout the concert Andy and Leslie stayed in this position.

It hardly seemed like two hours had passed, but it had and now the couple was slow dancing together at Kim's Blue Lights in the basement party on Herkimer Street. The Blue Lights made enough light as Andy and Leslie swayed to the music of Jerry Butlers' "Your Precious Love."

When Butler sang, the couples moved slower and touched each other intimately. When he got to the part of being "so lonely and so blue" there was enough heat generated to run the electricity in Bedford-Stuyvesant for a week.

Midnight Love.

Andy and Leslie walked down Green Street to her house. He walked to the iron gate and stopped. Leslie opened the gate and looked at Andy.

"What an evening."

"It was."

Andy pulled her close. He wanted to rhyme a love thought but was out of words.

The kiss was long.

Chapter Eleven

Andy reached, pulled the collar on his jacket up and around the back of his neck. He walked down the street away from Leslie's house. The light from the street lamps created shadows and lighted areas along Green Street. He took a deep breath and let out a sigh as he turned the corner and headed toward Broadway.

He didn't notice the men sitting in the car. They watched him as he passed the car, heading toward the corner. As he passed, the car door opened. Quickly, two men stepped out of the car and lunged at Andy.

First came the hard thud, as a fist almost knocked the breath out of Andy's chest. As he was falling to the cement, another fist caught him in the side. Andy was dazed. His legs buckled. He crumbled onto the cement. He felt a kick in the stomach, like hot lead eating at him. He looked up and recognized Peter Patterson.

Andy faded in and out of consciousness. He felt his body move, but not under its own power. He heard a car door slam and felt his head snap back against the front seat.

Andy heard Peter say, "Next time you won't get up!"

Ben Cain drove the ford slowly down Gates Avenue, cut through Boykin Drive until he reached Lafayette Avenue. He stop the car in front of the slap-board house. Peter jumped out the back seat and Ben the front. Both helped a groggy Andy up the stairs to the second floor apartment.

Andy felt himself being dumped into a straight-backed chair, in a dimly lit room. He felt his head roll from side to side. He tried to clear his thoughts. That came when Ben threw a jar of cold water in his face.

Andy opened his eyes with a gun in his face.

Peter smiled.

Andy heard a click.

Peter pushed the gun forward and it touched Andy's temple.

"That chamber was empty." Peter pulled the trigger, cocking it, getting it ready to send a bullet into Andy's head.

Ben laughed.

Peter pulled the trigger and again there was a click from the empty chamber.

Andy's forehead flushed out sweat as his heart skipped a beat.

Peter pulled the gun away from Andy's head and laid it on a table. "That was the appetizer."

Ben slapped his thigh and laughed out loud.

"Now…here comes the main course." Peter picked up a needle with a long silver tip. "You've had it too good. Everybody loves and protects Andy…and hates me. Well, I hate you. You've got everything going for you. I'm going to put a stop to all that favoritism."

Andy watched as Peter squeezed the base and liquid oozed from the tip. "No! ... No!" Ben grabbed Andy from the back and held him down.

Peter ignored his cries, moved forward and punctured Andy's right arm with the needle. The liquid flooded into Andy's veins.

Golda worried. It wasn't like Andy not to call or let them know if he was going to be late. And with the Towns shooting, she was on edge.

"Stop pacing," Marvs said.

"I can't help it."

"He'll be alright."

"Something is wrong."

Andy opened his eyes. He tried to move, but his body ached. He tried to figure out what happened, but his mind was still engulfed in a fog. He heard voices. He tried to speak. Somebody was restraining him.

"Try not to move young man." A policeman looked into his face. "Somebody roughed you up…can you speak?"

"Yeah." Andy sat up, holding his ribs. He felt a little dizzy, then the stinging caused him to grab his right arm.

"How'd you get here?" Andy asked the police.

"Somebody called the precinct and said to come to the corner of Green and Broadway, that a man was dead. You've be unconscious for a while. How're you feeling? We're going to take you to Kings County for observation and then call your home. We'll need a statement...Do you know who did this...?"

"I...No, No I don't.," Andy hesitated, still holding his right arm.

The phone rang close to two in the morning. Golda yanked the receiver out the base. "Oh, my God...Can we come and get him?"

Marvs and Golda grabbed their coats. Golda was the first out the door and Marvs followed, locking the apartment door.

Sister Love heard the noise and came to the door to investigate. "It's Andy...he's in the emergency room at Kings County. Somebody tried to beat him up."

"First Towns, now Andy." Sister Love closed the door as Marvs passed, following Golda down the steps.

Peter Paterson peeped through the crack in the door as Marvs closed the front door. He smiled. When he heard the door close, he looked to see if Trina was sleep, then he closed the apartment door, walked out onto Gates Avenue, toward Nostrand Avenue, turned the corner and headed toward Lafayette Avenue. He'd meet his partner, Ben Cain, to finish getting the dope for distribution.

The twenty-minute ride seemed like an hour, but they got to the door of the emergency room safely. Marvs was a good driver.

Golda and Marvs walked into the emergency room and saw the usual Saturday night Brooklyn carnage. Wounds from gun shots and knives had caused damage to many people. Red was a dominant color seeping through clothing.

"Marvs."

"Relax, Golda."

They weaved through all the bodies and headed to the window and a nurse. "We're looking for our son Andy Pilgrim, who was brought here by a policeman."

"Well lady the police have brought a lot of people here, some shot, some cut and some dead…"

Golda was about to explode when Marvs grabbed her arm. "Please miss…"

The nurse looked at the couple. "Let me check my records…yeah, he has some bruised ribs and a lump on his head, but he'll be alright. I'll take you to him."

She opened a door, Golda and Marvs walked through, and followed the nurse to a small area with white plastic curtain in front. She pulled the curtain and there was Andy with a white bandage wrapped around his chest and a band-aid under his eye.

"Andy." Golda rushed to her son. She wanted to hug him, but didn't because of the injury.

"Thank you," Marvs said to the nurse.

"He'll be alright…give him some aspirin. We gave him some penicillin and treated the wounds. He can go home."

Golda threw the shirt around Andy and Marvs followed her as they headed out of the emergency room. They walked briskly. Marvs opened the back door for Andy and the front for Golda. He got behind the steering wheel, turned the key and when the car purred he pulled away from the curb.

"What happened baby?" Golda turned toward Andy.

"I left Leslie's and then the next thing I knew I was jumped."

"Oh my God."

"Why?" Marvs asked.

"I don't know." Andy paused. "I saw Peter."

Golda froze and Marvs stared ahead as he drove down Bedford Avenue.

"Are you sure?" Marvs asked.

"Before I passed out, he said next time you won't get up."

Andy didn't tell his parents all that happened. He rubbed his right arm and kept quiet. He didn't know what Peter put in his arm, but he'd find out.

"Something has to be done or he's going to kill you." Marvs said.

"We've got to move or do something," Golda said.

"We're not running. Don't mention this to anybody. We'll decide what we have to do," Marvs said.

Andy looked out the window. "I'll have a day to recover. I can't miss any classes at school. I hope I'm well enough to speak at church tomorrow. Graduation is coming up and I'll be out of here soon enough."

"I hope so." Golda sighed.

Chapter Twelve

The red brick row house sat in the middle of Lafayette Avenue, three blocks from Gates Avenue and the four-hounded block. Two windows on the first floor and two on the second floor were boarded up with plywood in the front facing the street. In the back, the first floor windows covered with plywood and plastic. The upper floor windows had no glass, so Peter could look out on the back lots.

Peter sat at a table with two others from the neighborhood, putting cocaine into a plastic zip lock bag so small that you could fit the head of a lead pencil inside it. There were plastic bags ranging in size from the size of a thumb to an ordinary sized freezer bag. Now, the two drug dealers were putting the cocaine into bags for distribution.

The phone rang.

"Yeah, Ben and I scared Andy, I put a little something in his arm...OK." Peter slammed the receiver back into the base.

"Hole the bag still," Peter ordered, filling each bag with its lethal contents, then zipping the bag and placing it into containers that would be carried to drop off points.

"I'm trying," Ben yelled back.

"How's the recruiting? Peter asked.

"Cool," Ben said. "I went into the high school and got with some special education kids. Randall was very helpful in getting a place near the boiler room where we could meet. They don't know better, and they'll distribute the stuff."

"Good," Peter said. "We've expanded our business."

"Do you think we ought to lay low since we scared Towns and Andy?"

"No, we keep the heat up." Peter continued filling the bags.

Chapter Thirteen

Andy rolled over in his bed, sore and worried. His face was bruised and his right arm was sore. He didn't know if Peter had put heroine in his veins. Andy cried as he though about what could happen to his life.

He cringed when he visualized all those heroine addicts dozing on the corners and urinating on themselves. Andy prayed.

He knew he would speak at the Holiness Church around the corner on Nostrand Avenue in the afternoon. He didn't want to disappoint Elder Frank George.

Andy struggled out of bed and made his way to the kitchen. Each step gave him new confidence and strength. He made it to the refrigerator, opened the door and got out some milk and a piece of his mother's lemon pie.

The kitchen clock said it was noon.

"Up Andy?"

"Yes 'em."

"You feel like going to church? We went to morning service and said that you might speak at this afternoon's service."

"I'm going to speak."

"OK, we'll leave around two."

"I'll be ready." Andy walked to his room. He sat in the windowsill and watched the traffic. A cold chill chased him to his bed. He stretched across the bed and closed his eyes.

Golda called to him around one and Andy showered, dressed in his navy blue suit and light blue tie. He looked sharp. The swelling in his face wasn't too obvious.

When he walked into the living room, Marvs and Golda were dressed.

"Very handsome" Golda said.

Andy smiled.

They walked out of the apartment, down the steps and onto Gates Avenue. They crossed the street onto Nostrand Avenue. Nearing the church, well-dressed members were walking into the building. The woman wore the bright yellow, red and blue hats, tilted to the side. Talking softly at the entrance. Men, in their blue, black and pin-stripped suits, adjusted their ties.

Andy's elbow proved very useful as Golda walked, breathing a little heavy, up the steps.

"Praise the Lord," said Elder Frank, one of the leaders in the church and a fan of Andy who coached him and Peter on a basketball team at Public School 305. "It's good to see you Andy."

"It's good to be here Elder Frank," Golda said. "My boy is going to graduate from college in a few months and then become a sportswriter."

"Congratulations," Elder Frank said. "Make us proud. And Andy why didn't you drag some of your heathen friends to church."

"I promise next time I come to church, I'll drag many as I can."

Both smiled.

They walked into the sanctuary. It was big, with stained glass windows on the open side. The closed side was attached to the Laundromat. The ceiling was high. The altar was impressive with vases of live flowers in the front of the pulpit. The choir loft was in the back of the sanctuary, and filled with flowers.

Marvs, Golda and Andy sat down in the third row from the front in the center aisle. Andy took the bible from his mother and looked at the passage he would read to the congregation.

It was time for the service. The minister moved from his chair in the back of the pulpit to the microphone. A hush came over the people.

And then the choir started with "Precious Lord."

It was slow as the lead singer started with, "Precious Lord, take my hand, lead me on and let me stand. I am tired. I am weak. I am worn..."

Golda looked at Andy and held back tears. She prayed.

The choir finished with, "...lead me home." The congregation responded with "Amen" echoing harmoniously.

"Amen!" said Minister Charles. "Elder Frank will introduce the young man who will read the scripture lesson."

Elder Frank walked from the left side of the pulpit to the microphone, "Give our Choir another Amen!"

"Amen," could be heard from all parts of the church.

"And now we'll hear from a young man who grew up in the church," Elder Frank said. "He could've joined the rest of the gang members and dope dealers, but because of a strong mother and father, he's a quality person. Mr. Andy Michael Pilgrim will now read the scripture lesson."

Andy eased past his mother and father. Golda squeezed his hand lightly. She passed him the Bible. He smiled at her and walked to the pulpit. He approached the pulpit and gave Elder Frank a strong handshake. He looked over the congregation and found his mother and father's faces.

He opened the bible, spoke clearly and distinctly, "My text is from the Old Testament, the Book of Ecclesiastics. Chapter Three verses one to eight. And now the word of the Lord: To the heaven..." Andy read all eight verses.

Andy looked at the last verse, "A time to love, and a time to hate; a time of war and a time of peace," then slowly closed the bible. He held it high in his outstretched hands.

"The Word of the Lord, for the people of God," Andy said.

"Thanks be to God," the congregation responded.

Andy started to walk from the podium, but then he turned and walked back to the microphone. "May I say something?"

"Speak, young man," the minister said, a bit bewildered.

Andy looked on the anxious faces and focused on his mother and father. All eyes were on Andy. This didn't bother him.

"When I was reading that last verse, I was thinking about my life. I feel that there is always a time for love in this world: the love of a mother and a father and the love of God. When we walk the streets, death can come anytime. Whether it's the slow death of heroine addiction or a bullet in the head. We must stand for something. I will walk as straight a path as I can with the help of God."

Andy walked from the pulpit back to his seat. Andy prayed as he rubbed his right arm.

"Praise the lord," the minister said. "Praise the Lord"

Marvs and Golda hugged Andy. After the service, plenty of people came up to Andy. Some hugged Marvs and Golda, many others hugged Andy.

Chapter Fourteen

Andy was sore from the attack on Saturday night. He could move, but had trouble breathing. For a couple of days he was worried about going into the army and didn't realize that he needed an expensive book to finish his Eighteenth-Century Novels class. He didn't have the money.

His parents gave him as much money as they could but sometimes it was a struggle. Sister Love gave him money for extras. Andy turned his face to the wall. If it wasn't facing the Army, it was overcoming problems finishing his final year at City College.

The door creaked and Andy turned to see his stepfather, Marvs, step into the room. He was short, 5-8, with some extra pounds around the waist. His dark skin glistened in the light from the street. He had a way with him that reminded you of a college-educated person. He spoke English with a distinctive voice and his knowledge of the world impressed everybody who stepped into his yellow cab.

He was fully dressed, moneychanger on his side, ready to hit the streets of Manhattan.

"Where you going so early?"

Andy raised up on his pillow.

"I'll meet you at the bookstore at eight. I'm going to work the streets for a couple of extra hours so I can get the money. I hope you feel better."

Marvs stepped further into the room before retreating back through the door.

"Thanks..."

"I told you as long as you were going to college, we'd do anything to help you...be right in front of the bookstore."

"I will."

Marvs closed the door and Andy heard him walk down the steps.

Andy leaned back on the pillow and thought how fortunate his mother was in finding a good man to take care of her child. They escaped an abusive situation in Bush Chapel, Georgia. And found somebody to build a life.

Andy said a prayer of thanks.

Chapter Fifteen

The soreness in his shoulder from the gunshot wound made Towns cringe when he sat up in his chair. A few days at home and the hurt still caused him to labor at doing simple tasks, like raising a glass of water to his lips. He was getting better. At least this time he didn't spill half of the soda on his shirt. For the moment he felt safe in Queens.

The phone rang, startling Towns. He jumped, pulling his sore muscles so hard they twitched and ached. He reached for the phone through the pain barrier.

"Yes?"

Towns wanted to grunt from the pain, but didn't give any indication of the pain. "The money will be there...I'll call later. Did you scare Pilgrim? You what?"

Towns put the phone in the receiver and leaned back in the chair. He closed his eyes. A cold chill made him shiver as he realized Peter stuck Andy with the needle and put dope in his veins...heroine. He opened his eyes, adjusted his position so he could flip the radio. The soothing sounds of the Motown songs playing on WDAS kept him company. As he eased back in the chair, the Temptation's song "Just My Imagination came over the airwaves.

Towns dozed.

He thought of his close encounter at the Brooklyn Brownstone when he turned around and faced that gun. He knew who shot him, but he couldn't get a clear view of the gunman. All he'd felt was pain and then he was out.

With his recovery he'd closed the deal on 423 Gates Avenue, tearing the building down and make money. The gunshot wouldn't stop him from completing the deal that would change the appearance of that block.

Imagination had got him this far in life, where he owned properties in Brooklyn and Queens. After the shooting, he'd moved his office to Queens...can't trust those folks over on Gates Avenue anymore, but it wouldn't be long before it didn't matter what they thought.

Towns reached forward and turned the radio off. The pain caused him to stop in mid-reach, falling back into the chair. He drifted in a light sleep, then it became deeper. His sleep was sound and the phone ringing surprised him. He lunged forward, sending sharp pain surging throughout his body. He grabbed the phone and pulled it to his ear and then let it drop to the floor.

Chapter Sixteen

Randall walked from the subway at Nostrand and Fulton Streets to 423 and made his way up the steps to his apartment where he dialed Towns' number and waited for him to answer the phone.

"Next time the bullet will be in you heart!" Randall said and hung up the phone.

He sat down in his chair, smiled and slipped into deep thought. It would be a long day.

There was tension in the air at Bedford-Stuyvesant. The residents of 423 were feeling it from the pressure of Towns and his financial games, but there was a larger uneasiness that was building to a point of no return. All it would take was a spark and the polarized community would ignite into a riotous situation.

Andy stood outside the City College bookstore in the cool, breezy morning air. He waited on Convert Avenue as his stepfather drove toward him. Andy walked to the curb.

Marvs rolled down the window and smiled. "Here's the money, plus ten more to buy yourself something...and keep working hard so you can graduate in June."

"Thanks...I'll make you proud."

"Why all those people making signs?" Marvs pointed in the direction of Finley Hall.

"They're talking about shutting down the school."

"What!"

"'Power To The People' is the cry on campus the radical students are using to get everybody fired up."

"Well, I hope you're not involved."

"Nope, I just want to get out of here...but I'm sympathetic to their cause."

"Just don't get yourself in trouble."

"I won't."

Marvs pulled away from the curb and headed to midtown Manhattan and hopefully a fare to Kennedy airport to make some more money.

Andy walked to the bookstore and got his book for his class, plus a copy of Jane Austen's novel, *Pride and Prejudice.* He wanted to read again about the Bennett family's five daughters. He walked up the hill to Finley Center, the student center on the South Campus. There, he'd find out the latest news, concerning the planned shutdown of City College, Columbia and some of the other schools in New York City.

Chapter Seventeen

Mother Nature's high-pitched laughter could be heard, not only in Golda's ear, but also across the house. Her husband Sweet Thang yelled to Golda about coming over later that day to see her and Marvs. Mother Nature's nasal inflective voice was distinctive.

"You'll be careful down on Gates…the word on the streets is there will be trouble."

"People are always talking about trouble on the streets from the militants…"

"This time there is something to it…trust me."

"I hope not, not here on our quiet street."

"Well, keep your eyes and ears open."

"I will."

Mother Nature walked into the living room. "I hope Golda and Marvs will be all right down there…"

"Stop worrying, they're smart. At the first sign of trouble they know they have a place to stay here."

"Since those kids called you 'Sweet Thang', you think you're something on a stick."

"I just called them kids my 'Sweet Things' and they turned around and called me 'Sweet Thang' and everybody has picked up my name… well, it's true I am a Sweet Thang, but you know I'm just an everyday person."

"Damn, you can still talk too much."

"Don't curse."

"I will, if you won't."

"Hurry up and get dressed so we can get to the Cocktail Sip."

Chapter Eighteen

Sweet Thang relaxed on the bed as Mother Nature dressed in the bathroom. It didn't seem that long ago that he was in South Vietnam fighting for the cause of justice. He was an Air Force fire fighter and his job caused him nightmares. That's why he spent most of his days drinking himself into a stupor.

He rested his hands behind his head on his pillow. Sweet Thang closed his eyes and he was back at Da Nang air field where the sky was filled with the flames exploding from the back of the B-52 bomber. A surface-to-air missile hit the jet and it limped to the airfield. Sweet Thang and the rest of the ground fire-fighting unit waited for the jet to land.

Sweet Thang watched as the jet wobbled from side to side, descending faster than normal, and as it neared the ground, with landing wheels deployed, the pilot was able to keep the nose steady, but sparks rained as the nose touched the cement runway. The sliding created a screeching that was more irritating than someone scratching fingernails on a chalkboard. Flames ate the plane.

As the jet came to a halt, Sweet Thang and the rest of the Fire Fighters sprinted toward the plane. They broke the doors down, rushing into the super-heated inferno that was raging in the interior to see if anyone survived. They moved around the open areas. Sweet Thang stepped into something soft. He looked down and realized his right foot had crushed the chest of an airman and was pushing against the floor. He brought his foot up hard and sprinted out of the burning airplane. All he wanted to do was just run. He couldn't stop running.

He didn't realize that he was beating against the wall, which he regularly did, when he was having one of his war-centered nightmares. His right fist kept hitting the wall harder. This finally brought Mother Nature into the bedroom.

She grabbed his hands.

"Sweet Thang, Sweet Thang?"

His wild rage kept his head tossing on the pillow.

Sweet Thang opened his eyes, glaring at Mother Nature.

"Stop it, you're dreaming again."

She sat on the bed behind him and continued rubbing his head. He calmed down and sat up on the bed. Twenty years in the Air Force had ended with Sweet Thang coming out with a drinking problem that was a result of the constant nightmares. Seeing the maimed and burned bodies and all that death had taken its toll.

"Get me a drink. I need to get my world clouded again so I won't have to think about all those horrible things."

"NO! You've got to drive and you will not drink and drive me any place in Brooklyn."

"I need one."

"So."

"But…"

"No, get dressed so we can go to the Cocktail Sip on time."

Mother Nature kissed him on the forehead and pulled him off the bed. She pushed him toward the bathroom. She walked into the living room and found the 45 record with Al Green's recording of "How to Mend a Broken Heart."

She put the record on the turntable and let it play over and over, while Sweet Thang dressed. She thought about how her family in Somerset, New Jersey didn't like her being with the man she loved, but she already told them that she loved the tall, skinny brown-sugar toned man with the pencil thin mustache.

Her family thought he wasn't light-complexioned enough or had enough money for her. They looked down on him, but Mother Nature loved him ever since they met at the Chock Full Onus restaurant on Fulton Street. He came in for a cup of coffee and went out with her heart.

"Ready."

She looked up at the 6-2, skinny, but very handsome man standing in the doorway.

"Come here Sweet Thang and give me some brown sugar."
They kissed.
"Ready to party?"
"Born ready."

Chapter Nineteen

Marvs moved the coffee table away from the center of the living room, next to the floor model television. "Don't touch any of my furniture." Golda could look from the kitchen straight to the living room in the railroad apartment. There was a knock on the door and Reds, Willie Johnson and Johnny Thurmond entered the fourth-floor apartment.

This was the second Tuesday of the month and the regular rehearsal time of Marvs' gospel group.

"Yo Marvs," Willie Johnson almost doubled over laughing. "You won't believe what." Reds glared and shot back in his deep gravel bass voice. "I will..."

"Come on in and relax before I get started."

Willie and Johnny sat down on the couch. Reds found the love seat and wiped his face with the handkerchief that he always carried. Johnny stood and turned the volume down on the television.

"As I was saying..." Willie chuckled and looked at Reds. "Tell the world."

"Reds and one of his East New York cronies came out of Barbara's lounge on Fulton Street. Reds staggered, turned completely around and just sat down on the curb crying. Pretty soon a crowd of people gathered around Reds. See that white handkerchief that he always carries...well, he kept wiping his eyes and crying.

"Finally, one of those beat cops walked by and asked him what he was doing sitting on the curb crying. He blurted out that he was depressed. The cop told him to take his depressed ass and get off his curb or he'd take him to 79th precinct. Reds staggered until he saw a cab..."

"Willie, the only reason you found out was big-mouth Johnny was with me and told everybody..."

"Well, let's get ready for our rehearsal. We'll discuss the

crying man after we finish…"

"Marvs, not you too."

"No, not yet."

"And I thought you were my friend."

"I am…come on everybody, let's get ready to rehearse."

Marvs stood up and the rest of the group stood up with him. Marvs, Reds and Johnny stood up together while Willie, the lead singer, was to the left.

"Remember, when we get in Mt. Zion Baptist Church, we'd better perform. I told them we're going to do 'What A Friend We Have In Jesus.' Ready, One…Two…Three…let the church say 'Amen'…touch somebody next to you and tell them 'I found a friend and His name is Jesus.'

"Then, Willie will start and the rest of us will come in." Marvs gave the signal. "I'm so happy…What a friend we have in Jesus…all our sins and grief to bear…what a privilege, the Lord carries…take unto the Lord in Prayer…O what peace we often forfeit…O what needless pain we bear… it's all because we do not carry everything to God in prayer…can you find one so faithful…who will all our sorrows bear…Jesus already knows our every weakness…all you got to do is take it to the Lord in prayer."

Everybody bowed their heads and relaxed.

"Maybe this will be our big break." Willie plopped down on the seat.

"As long as we serve the Lord, all the rest of that stuff is extra,"Reds said. "I know I drink and one day the Lord will take that from me. I still serve him with my voice." Andy walked through, headed to the kitchen, as the group relaxed in the living room.

"Yo, Andy, I'm glad you didn't get drafted."

"Yo, I feel better. Sweet Thang told me some stories that didn't make me want to go over there and get involved in that shooting match."

"You don't need that," Reds said, wiping his forehead with that white handkerchief.

"Keep working in school and get a good job making lots of money."

"I will.' Andy kept walking toward the kitchen.

"Yo, Marvs. What's this I hear about a shooting in your building?"

"Yeah...somebody shot Jesse Towns the landlord, downstairs in the basement."

"Why?"

"He's playing his games and somebody will make him pay the piper for what he's doing trying to sell this Brownstone from right under us. The tenants are up in arms. The police came out looking for somebody, but the tenants were at work or out of the building. It could have been anybody in his building or a number of people on this block. He's got a lot of people ready to tear into his butt."

"What are you all going to do?"

"I don't know."

"We'll always find a place to stay."

"You'd better watch out for that guy Randall...I wouldn't trust him," Reds said, wiping the sweat off his forehead. "I heard some things at the bar where people know him from Virginia."

"He's always been nice to me and me family."

Chapter Twenty

Andy got off the "A" train at 125th Street and decided to walk the long way through the park to Convent Avenue. It was early in the morning and a cool breeze snapped at his face. His backpack was filled with books and he was ready for that Eighteenth Century novel exam.

As he walked up the hill, he heard the chants. They grew louder as he neared the campus. He saw the anti-war demonstrators standing in the middle of Convent Avenue. They were yelling to the Black and Puerto Rican students that were behind the cement brick wall.

Something was not right.

Andy climbed the hill and as he got closer, the noise level got louder. He saw what he feared. The gate was chained and the grates were covered with anti-Vietnam war signs and posters. Students inside the gate kept up a running conversation with radical students, clerical workers and college administrators trying to get into the college.

For weeks the radicals had threatened to shut down The College to bring attention to the draft, the war, and plight of minorities at The College. Now, they finally had done it — shut down South Campus and the rest of the City College. Andy turned and saw a local television news crew and he knew this would be one of the lead items on the Six O'Clock News.

Andy walked up convent Avenue and to the intersection that separated north and south campus. The radicals blocked the entrance to every major building. Shepard Hall, the main Chancellor and the rest of the deans couldn't get to their offices. With City College shut down, it was a crisis situation like Columbia University and other colleges across America. The next step was up to the University.

Chapter Twenty-one

For five weeks the long overdue Black and Puerto Rican cultural revolution swept across the Campus.

The City College of New York was shutdown.

Everyday people visited the campus to see if the crisis was over and, hopefully, get back to the business of education.

Some people blamed the radical students and others blamed the administration. Everybody agreed there was a generation gap, perhaps several. Most students didn't hesitate to add that the only way change would come was through violence and extreme measures, such as the take over of a university.

Now, everybody waited to see if the administration would call in the police to clear the campus or negotiate a deal that would peacefully end the crisis. Inside the walls, where the students barricaded themselves, there was tension, because of the fear of violence.

The question everybody asked: "What would be the resolution of the events that began five weeks ago with the take over of the Black and Puerto Rican students? Would they get their demands for higher minority admissions to City College in the fall?"

The day was warm as Andy made his daily trip up the hill to The College. His mother was worried, because she didn't want Andy to get involved with anything that might put him in the emergency room at Kings County Hospital.

Andy edged toward the gate and pushed aside one of the homemade signs and peered through the openings of the black cast iron gate. In three months he hoped he would graduate and get the job in sports writing. The offer from the World Journal-Tribune looked good, but with no diploma, there wouldn't be any job. He preferred Washington D.C. For now, Andy's plan was the prisoner of the City College lockout.

He moved his face closer to the cold steel gate. From inside somebody touched his shoulder. He pivoted quickly. "Mario Hamilton!"

"Yo...Yo...Cool it Brooklyn boy."

"Man, you scared me."

"Sorry."

"I thought you were one of those radical students taking out a little revenge..."

"Nope, just your buddy from the Bronx."

"Man...I'm worried."

Andy turned away from the fence and saw his friend Charles, who was waiting for him to finish talking with Mario.

"You, being a senior without a diploma will not sit well with most employers," Mario said.

"Yeah, I've traveled from Brooklyn, four years, to Harlem to get my diploma. I've already missed five weeks and what will happen next. I can't sing... I can't dance...I'm not going to do. My parents have sacrificed so much for me and now to give it away doesn't seem fair.

"Yet, I agree with all the five demands. I agree with change. However, I do not agree with some methods used on campus. I don't go along with violence and class disruptions, yet, I know there must be change. As I see it, there will not be change.

"It's so pathetic, out of some 20,000 students, only 500 showed up last week for the student convocation to help solve the crisis. I don't think many people in this school really care."

Mario, who was supposed to finish up his pre-law program in the summer, moved closer to the fence. Andy turned to nod to Charles and looked past him down Convent Avenue and Harlem. Andy turned and faced Mario.

"I don't go along with all the violence either, but what has happened here at The College has happened in the eyes of many people. Something good has come out of it already...even though we did it the extreme way.

"America is alarmed and America is spiritually dead. Blacks and Puerto Ricans will bring the nation back and give the white man one more chance at salvation."

While Mario and Andy were talking, one of the leaders of the "take over" called Mario.

"Come here!"

Mario and Andy recognized Hiram Henry's voice. Both smiled and moved toward the fence. Andy reached his hand through the gate and gave his friend the Black-power handshake.

"Brothers are you with us?"

Andy didn't answer, but waited a moment. "We're fighting the battle out here." Andy spoke up, so Henry could hear him, as he moved away from Mario and the fence.

Mario moved inside the barricade toward Finley Hall. A group of students were listening to Henry's voice.

"You know we made our demands many months ago...there wasn't a reaction from the administration. So, we took over the campus. We did it because we were ignored! Guess what...we got their attention.

"We, Blacks and Puerto Ricans, were noticed as a result of our taking over the campus in non-violent way. Dr. King was right, when you demonstrate peacefully your opponent can't handle it. In my eyes, it was good that it happened, maybe not the rioting and burning, but this is the result of frustration being held so long..."

Mario left the crowd, listening to Henry, and came over to the fence to talk with Andy before he left campus.

"In Bed-Sty something is brewing, I can feel it." Andy moved closer to the iron gate. "If something isn't done, it's going to explode."

"Hey, the south Bronx isn't far behind. It's just a sign of the times...people are afraid of change and when it happens, they will get violent. Emotions are frozen in anger mode and can't be changed."

"Yeah, but I hope these changes we're making today will

make black, white, and brown people in the future learn from these mistakes, so this will never happen again."

Mario stared at Andy. "The politicians won't let that happen because a political issue as volatile as this will be used for their personal gains. Each generation must fight the battle again and again, whether it's in the sixties, seventies, eighties or even the nineties."

"I'm afraid you're right," Andy said.

Mario moved from the gate. "You and Charles get out of here, I see people with cameras. Fight the battle outside these walls...Power to the people!"

Mario moved toward Finley where Henry was speaking to the crowd, while Charles and Andy walked down Convent to the subway. Andy jumped on the southbound "A" train to Brooklyn and Charles got on the northbound to the Bronx.

Chapter Twenty-two

Andy sprinted up the subway steps at 85th Street and Central Park West and entered a different Manhattan. The day was cool, but the bright sunshine warmed his soul. A few moments ago he was in the heart of Harlem and now he was on Manhattan's prosperous upper West Side. He jogged across the street to the park entrance and walked to his favorite spot, a large granite outcrop that gave him a perfect view of the midtown office towers. He could turn in any direction and look uptown to Harlem, east toward Greenwich Village.

It was a good view that offered Andy an opportunity to dream and get into his thoughts. Now, the phantoms that haunted his soul could take on a real form. His memories and doubts about the failure could take on personalities that at first attacked and then soothed his inner being.

Andy sighed and stared at the Manhattan skyline. He wanted to walk from City College to this spot, but he just wasn't in the mood. He'd seen the poverty of Harlem and how, as he moved south, the streets were transformed into the moneyed West Side of Central Park.

On his personal rock he reflected on the past few months as his mind went from the morning he went before the draft board to the shooting in the Brownstone and finally to the take over of City College. It was May. In a few weeks he would be a part of City College's graduation at Madison Square Garden.

Many things were happening, and yet, the most important thing was his future job as a sportswriter. Would all his goals and dreams be put on hold? If Black and Puerto Rican students didn't release the grip on City College, a lot of his fellow seniors' future plans would vanish.

And then there was Leslie.

Andy stood up and clasped his hands around the back of

his head. "Sometimes, I wonder if the good moments are worth the anxiety of waiting by the phone. I must evaluate our relationship before I get deeper in love with Leslie. "Questions must be answered. Those eyes and that personality are captivating. I must decide between what is true and what is false. My feelings must find a true path. I can say it is love, but where would it lead me?

"I must get answers...I'll spend time in prayer. I will meditate on my feelings. I really love Leslie...I'll have to make some difficult choices. It'll be tough choosing loneliness over the comfort of being with another person. I'll either fall deeper in love or get over her. I want more than a platonic relationship. Our love will either evolve or disappear.

Andy turned in the direction of Harlem. He hoped it would take his thoughts off Leslie. But it didn't.

"Leslie and I have become close. We share many ideas. We will exchange commitment jewelry: a heart and a key. We'll break it together...she'll keep the key to my heart."

Andy reached up to his neck, unbuttoned the first two buttons. "I trust Leslie with my heart. I believe in her because if you don't have trust, respect and commitment, you don't have a relationship."

He reached and rubbed the spot where Peter had stuck him with the needle. Andy felt cold and yet he had hot flashes. Emotions surged at a rapid pitch in his body. He was trying to figure out what Peter had put in his veins. It was some kind of drug.

He felt deep in his gut that the chance of becoming an addict was not automatic. It would take more than one time before his body would crave it. There was the chance, but that would depend on his body chemistry, his heredity and his background. Andy felt some pain as he hit the hard rock with his fist.

Andy knew it wasn't cocaine, because your body can't reproduce that extreme high...a craving would result. He didn't feel depressed and didn't want another dose. If it were

LSD he would have passed could nine and saw and felt things that weren't there.

He jumped straight up. It was heroin that was circulating in his veins. All the pictures of people screaming in pain, body aching, diarrhea, muscle cramps and wanting to kill for another dose flashed in his mind.

Andy knew he had another battle. He felt that if he didn't fight, he'd lose everything. He clinched his sore fist, gritted his teeth and decided he'd fight for his life.

Andy buttoned his shirt and jumped down from the rock. He walked back from his personal meditation rock and turned down Central Park West. He was in a good pace, enjoying the surroundings when he heard the car horn. That shouldn't have made him look, because cars honk their horns all the time in Manhattan. He recognized his father's cab.

Marvs pulled over to the curb.

"Hop in...I'm headed to the garage and home."

"Good." Andy opened the door and got in beside his father.

"Campus still closed?"

"Yeah...nobody can get in or out. I hope something breaks soon, 'cause I want to graduate in June."

"It will."

Marvs headed to downtown Manhattan, followed his normal route to the Brooklyn Bridge which put him right at his garage in downtown Brooklyn, not far from the Williamsburg section. Marvs and Andy switched from the cab to the family car.

Home was a few minutes away.

Chapter Twenty-three

Andy thought about his mother's favorite saying as he walked up the steps to the apartment. Marvs and Andy carried brown bags filled with groceries from Key Foods on Nostrand Avenue.

His mother always said, "Reach for the highest bush where you will find the best berries."

All his life Andy has reached for the best, whether it was winning an elementary school spelling contest or waiting counters at his summer job with the Chock-Full O'Nuts restaurant on 34th Street in Manhattan. Andy knew it would take his best to fight off the possibility of addiction.

Now, he watched as Marvs neared the top of the stairs and knocked on the door. "Wait, let me help you," Andy called out. "I've got the door...your Mamma will be there waiting for us."

"I know."

"You leaving us soon."

"No."

Andy raced in front of Marvs and knocked on the door.

"I'm going to stay home unless I find a job in Philly or Washington...but I've got feelers to work with the World-Journal Tribune and as a copy boy with The New York Times.

"What I really want to do is write sports with a big city newspaper. When you reach for the stars, you've got to start at the very bottom. I want a firm foundation so I can build something that will last. I don't want something that will quickly go away...it must last."

"Good," Marvs said, as he heard Golda's footsteps near the door.

"About time you two got home, put those bags down on the kitchen table."

Marvs moved toward the kitchen as Andy walked in the

door. Golda kissed Andy. He moved in front of her, walking toward the kitchen, putting his grocery bags down.

"Mamma."

"I'll kiss you as long as you're my baby, so stop squirming and trying to run away. I don't stop you when you come into our room and kiss me and Marvs on the cheeks when you think we're sleep..."

"I'll call you when it's time for supper."

Andy walked to his room and closed the door. Marvs and Golda put the groceries up in the cabinet above the sink and stove.

"How'd it go today?"

"Good."

Marvs walked to the living room and opened his bag where he kept his moneychanger, taxi-driver identification.

"I've got something for Andy."

He walked to the kitchen and handed Golda a post card with the black diva Pearl Bailey's signature over her picture from the Broadway show, "Hello Dolly."

"He'll love this."

Golda gingered the post card, which showed Pearl Bailey in the famous Harmonica Garden scene, from the musical, where she strutted her stuff with the show stopping "Hello Dolly" number.

"I heard something on the streets... it wasn't good."

"What?"

Golda put the autograph picture on a napkin and laid it on the table. "Let's go into the living room so we can sit down and talk."

"With all this talk of Black power in the air, the rumor is that the inner cities are going to explode."

"What you mean?"

"Riots!"

"Here on Gates Avenue."

"Yes Golda, even here on Gates Avenue people feel put down and ready to do violent things. Listen to the news everyday. Down in Birmingham people are bombing churches with little children in them, out in Chicago young leaders are being killed and in Harlem people resent everybody. Even Andy was affected when City College closed."

"Let's watch the news and see what's going on."

"There's always something going on, just look out the window on Gates Avenue and you'll see everything you need. Marvs, what's that truck doing across the street?"

Marvs pushed himself up from the couch and moved toward the window. He stopped in his tracks.

He stared at the Repo Man.

Chapter Twenty-four

Towns knew he was taking a big risk putting pressure on the people in the Brownstone. He wanted to show the residents he meant business. From the street, he could see the people looking out their windows.

In the front of the Brownstone the demolition team was poised to make a move toward 423. Towns, who everybody called the "Repo Man", even had the Brooklyn police with him on the sidewalk across the street. Towns, the demolition team and the police were poised. After the shooting, he was ready to force the people out of the building and tear it down.

Crowds of people gathered, then more of the residents from the block showed up to jeer Towns and the police. Traffic crawled along Gates Avenue. The residents stood on the stoop and yelled across at Towns.

Towns walked toward them with the two policemen as bodyguards. "I've got an eviction order for everybody in the building."

"You got what!" someone yelled from the building.

"A court order."

"For what?"

"You have 72 hours to clear out of the building or it will be torn down around you."

Marvs stepped toward Towns and took the paper out of his hand. "You didn't have guts enough to come to us, but you had to make a scene in front of the entire neighborhood. You won't get away with this."'

Marvs turned toward the Brownstone, but then looked back at Towns, then turned toward the stoop leaving Towns and he two policemen in the middle of the street.

Marvs stopped, turned and faced Towns. "I just hope you didn't set my son up to be attacked."

Towns stepped toward Marvs. "Would I do that?"

"I wouldn't trust you. Nothing better happened to him." Marvs turned and walked toward the stoop.

Towns turned, looked over his shoulder, walked across the street.

Chapter Twenty-five

Golda opened the door and the people from the building followed Marvs back into the Pilgrim's living room. It was crowded, but everybody found a space to either sit or stand. The living room was as crowded as any rush hour that filled the B-52 bus with people coming from downtown Brooklyn. Everybody was in the room except for John Randall.

"Well Marvs, what does this mean?"

Trina Paterson looked worried as she walked into the apartment closing the door behind her.

"Simple, we'd better find some place to go in three days or our furniture and belongings will be sitting on the sidewalk."

Sister Love sat down hard on the couch and slapped the carved wood end of the couch with her hand.

"Where's John Randall, this will affect him also."

Marvs closed the door. He looked across the room at Golda, Trina, Sister Love, Jon and Andy. Marvs wondered what was going to happen.

Before Marvs could sit down there was a hard knock on the door.

"Who's here?"

"It's me."

"Me, who?"

Marvs answered, peeping out of the peephole.

"Randall." Marvs opened the door.

"I figured I'd better come."

"Towns is up to his old tricks," Golda said. "Marvs, what does that paper say?"

Marvs looked across the living room and at Golda with her worried look. It was the same one that greeted him when Andy was going for his Army physical and when he was in the emergency room.

Trina sat next to Golda holding her hand, while Sister Love

and Jon Raymond stood next to each other in the kitchen doorway. Andy was his usual pensive self as he walked back from his bedroom window after watching the crowd disperse.

Everybody watched Marvs as he read the papers. He walked and paced. Outside the B-52 bus made its regular stops.

Everything seemed normal.

Chapter Twenty-six

Under the watchful eye of the Brooklyn policemen, Towns got into his car and pulled away from the curb. He'd done it. If everything worked out, he'd get the fruits of all his work: money. Towns felt good. He was about to win. Nobody would keep him from his goal. He felt invincible.

Towns looked at the number 423 on the Brownstone and the policemen across the street. He smiled, turned the corner and drove up Marcy Avenue. The shadows on the block could cloak things, including a speeding bullet.

First, the glass shattered, forcing Towns to close his eyes and jerk himself down and away from the flying glass. He lost control. The car swerved right and just missed impacting a telephone pole. It came to an abrupt stop inches from the stoop of an apartment house.

Towns lifted his head off the front seat and looked around. He picked broken glass off his shirt. He peeped over the dashboard. His car was on the sidewalk. He'd just missed hitting a truck. The engine was running. He brushed the remaining broken glass off his pants.

He didn't know how, but he maneuvered the car between two parked cars, jumped the curb. Towns didn't get out, but kept picking the glass from around him and looking to see if somebody was coming after him. He'd just left a chaotic scene and nobody from there could have rushed around to Marcy Avenue to beat him to this spot.

Towns felt safe enough to sit up and look around. There were a few winos drinking in the small park and they weren't pointing guns. They were pointing the wine bottle to their mouths. The car's motor hummed. He put the car in reverse and backed onto Marcy Avenue.

Across the street, a man peeped over the top of a car and watched Towns pull off. He smiled.

Chapter Twenty-seven

Downtown Brooklyn and Fulton Street were crowded. People bumped into each other coming out of the Brooklyn Fox Theater. They strolled past the Dime Savings Bank and other shops along the Borough's busiest shopping area.

Andy walked out of the A&S Department store with a huge container of milk and an Apricot Danish that Sister Love had given him at the lunch counter. His hands were full and so he backed out the glass door hoping not to bump into anybody.

He turned, munching on his lunch, and headed for the movies to see the latest Sidney Poitier movie, "Lilies of the Field."

Andy needed this break to do some thinking about his future. It'd been two days, but it seemed like years. Andy felt his world was disintegrating. There was the draft board, the City College student lockout, Peter shooting drugs in his veins and now this crazy Towns trying to snatch the Brownstone from his family and friends. No wonder someone shot out his car window when he tried to have everybody evicted. Everybody felt Randall did it, but nobody was sure.

His father went to court, the next day, and got a court order that stopped Towns for a while from evicting everybody from the Brownstone. At least, he had a few hours to get things sorted out in his mind.

Andy felt his rib cage and the soreness was almost gone, but the chill of the attack was still there. Peter was after him and he didn't know how he was going to handle the situation.

Andy looked at the blue sky with this one cloud trying to blot out the sun. It seems when things were going good, there were people trying to destroy the happy mood.

Everyone at 423 was busy with their own problems, but few realized a bigger cloud was coming. The wind was building up strength to bring in a black cloud of discontent that was engulfing the country and Brooklyn was in the direct line of fire.

When the six o'clock television news came on, the visual images and news of riots in Detroit, Watts in Los Angeles and other American urban centers dominated the airwaves.

Andy passed three guys leaning on a car and one was putting his head through a car window listening to the radio.

"Something's going down in Bed-Sty soon." The man's dark skin couldn't hide the u-shaped scar on his right cheek. He wore green, blue and yellow attire. When his spoke his eyes flashed.

"What?" His friend responded in a loud whisper that could be heard above the noise from the passing cars.

"Did you hear Brother Stokely Carmichael the other night from Detroit? Well, he said there was no question of whether there is violence, but when..."

"I don't know about that, but I do know that up in Harlem brothers are sick of being treated like animals."

He turned, looked at Andy as he passed.

"Yo, young brother, people are getting ready for a change."

Andy turned.

"You be careful."

Andy smiled.

He continued, "We got to watch out for each other. I was in South Vietnam and I feel the same kind of attitude over here among the cops. I saw violence in Vietnam, and now in the streets of the inner-cities, you hear cops use words that American troops used in Vietnam...detainees and other things. It's how they treat us that make us react this way."

Andy smiled and kept on walking, give him a raised fist and verbal "Right On" to show his solidarity and that he was down with the movement. He looked and they were still having their discussion. Andy swallowed his last bit of Danish and downed the milk. He saw the movie theater come into view near Junior's Restaurant. It was across the street from the Carvel ice cream parlor. A Flying Saucer ice cream sandwich would taste good now, but he knew he wouldn't have time to indulge.

He passed the music store and was going straight to the movies, but he went back. When he opened the door, the clerk was putting in Petula Clark's hit song, "Downtown."

"May I help you?"

"No thanks, just lookin'."

Andy walked to the rack of singles, the latest 45 records. He flipped through some Al Green songs and then found the one for his mother, Joe Tex's song about the woman with the skinny legs.

"That?"

The clerk smiled.

"Please...it's for my parents. I don't listen to stuff like that."

"You want to hear it?"

"No!"

Andy handed the clerk a dollar and twenty-five cents. He got eleven cents change. He walked out the door and straight to the movie theater. Andy looked at the marquee listing for "Lilies of the Field" with Sidney Poitier who won the academy award. Andy paid two dollars and stepped into the world of make believe.

Chapter Twenty-eight

The B-52 city bus motored down Gates Avenue, letting passengers on and off at each corner. Andy pulled the cord, ringing the bell, alerting the bus driver that he was getting of at Nostrand and Gates Avenue.

When the bus pulled up to the curb, Andy stepped down in front of Mitchell's Drug Store. He carried the Joe Tex record in his hands and the memory of "Lilies of the Fields" in his mind. He sprinted across the street, turned right, past the fish market, Mr. Possum's candy store and then into the "Hair is Art" Barber shop.

Andy moved through the crowded shop and found a seat near the back under the pictures of Malcolm X and Martin Luther King. The four barber chairs were filled and customers who were waiting to claim one as it emptied. Behind the chairs a wall length mirror gave each customer a chance to examine that fresh cut.

Under the mirror was a counter extended the length of the room, filled with drawers. They were filled with clippers, hair lotions, hair creams, scissors, combs and other hair equipment organized neatly behind each of the four barber chairs.

"You're next."

Lenny pointed toward Andy.

"Good."

Andy smiled as Lenny finished giving the man a hairstyle call a Fade.

Andy looked around and listened as conversations about women, the poor play of the New York Mets and rumors of trouble in the streets of the inner cities dominated the room.

On the television, during the six o'clock evening news, black United States congressman Adam Clayton Powell from Harlem was talking about the problems occurring from the integration of schools in the south and the closed job market in the north.

"That Powell is something else. He tells it like it is," the old man said as he left the barbershop.

"You're right." Lenny continued to cut his customers hair.

"Everybody better listen, 'cause the only person keeping this nation from turning violent is Martin Luther King," said Paul, and the barber shaping a customer's mustache, in the chair next to Lenny.

One customer looked up from his JET magazine and pointed at the crowd in the barbershop. "I was at a meeting the other night on Amsterdam Avenue in Harlem and I heard Eldridge Cleaver talk to the brothers. He told 'em, "Take meaningful steps to get individual freedom. Those steps will be coming soon and you'd better get ready for the violence!"

"Anything going down here in Bed-Sty?" someone yelled from the back of the shop. "I'm hearing rumors."

"Rumors...I hope none of that rioting comes this way, I spent too much of my life building this business to see it go up in flames. We have a good block with hard working people," Lenny said. "When people riot it doesn't matter what the color, everything and everybody gets hurt.

"Don't tell me about freedom, I grew up in Virginia and here in Brooklyn it' just as bad..."

"What you mean?" Paul looked up after putting the finishing touches on his mustache.

"Just what I said." Lenny gave his customer a mirror so he could judge the cut. The customer moved his head from side-to-side, gave a nod in approval, then handed the mirror back to Lenny. He handed Lenny a ten-dollar bill, telling him to keep the change, and got up and left.

"Next."

Andy moved toward Lenny. He paused for a few seconds as Lenny knocked the hair off the chair.

"What style Mr. Pilgrim?"

"Low on the sides and high on the top with a part in the middle."

"That'll look good."

Andy looked around the barbershop and saw a lot of neighbors from the four hundred block. In a big city, a block is like a small town. Once you cross the street, you have friends and neighbors and also some that don't want to be part of the town. It felt good to see a lot of the people he'd come to know and like over the past nine years.

"I heard about the lockout." Lenny moved Andy's head so he could get a better angle for the clippers. "Did you ever get back to school?"

"Yeah...the police were going to storm the school, but the administration agreed to the ten demands and classes are normal again. Some of the student leaders have been arrested and I feel that something will still happen...it's still not over.

"I'll graduate in June, if nothing happens, with a degree in Journalism. I'm trying to get a job as a sportswriter."

"That's good...it's about time some of our young people get a chance at something good."

Lenny was over 6-3 with graying hair around the temples. He wanted to see young people from the neighborhood do well.

"Stay away from those gangsters in the streets, but I know your mamma and daddy and they'll keep you straight."

"You'd better believe it."

"I heard about the attack on you...Be careful."

"I will."

Andy glanced at the clock. It was close to seven and he knew he had to get home to do some studying for tomorrow's Shakespeare exam. That third act in Macbeth was tough. He wanted to get everything ready, because he wanted to see Leslie at her job when his classes at City College were over.

"Looking good Mr. Pilgrim." Lenny put the final touches on Andy's fresh cut. He brushed the excess hair from his head and splashed on some cologne. "That's for the ladies."

"One lady," Andy smiled.

"Who?"

"Leslie Groves from up near Gates and Broadway,"

Andy paid Lenny and gave him a generous tip. That's something Marvs had instilled in him. A cab driver needs tips to bring home extra money to his family. Those tips helped put him through college.

"Thanks." Lenny took the money. "Next...Andy be careful, 'cause I got a bad feelin' about things going on in the neighborhood."

"I will."

Andy closed the door, turned left and walk toward the middle of the block to 423. He opened the black Iron Gate, closed it behind him, and walked up the steps.

It seemed turmoil in the world had left him behind when he closed the gate. Andy looked up the steps and saw the gold-plated numbers on the door.

Home and a good night's rest would feel good.

Chapter Twenty-nine

The bright sunlight forced Andy to squint his eyes. He staggered up the steps of the BMT subway station at Brighton Beach. Andy walked the long block from the subway to Kingsborough Community College. The City University had taken the former Army barracks and turned them into a place to develop a two-year college.

It was a place where dreams developed for high school students without the grades to get into four-year colleges. It was students who needed help in developing basic reading and writing skills, came from afternoon study sessions and in the summer.

Andy passed dorms and classrooms overlooking the Atlantic Ocean. A cool breeze made Andy's walk easy. He looked to the fourth building and saw Leslie. They exchanged smiles, hugged and kissed.

Andy and Leslie walked to the beach, holding hands, and watching the blue-green waves slap rhythmically on the shoreline. Andy squeezed Leslie's hand.

"Your thoughts?"

Andy pulled Leslie's hand to his lips and gently kissed it.

"You."

"Really?"

"Then, what was the dude from the Bronx doing at your house last Sunday?"

Leslie smiled.

"You heard about that."

"Yeah...I know everything when it concerns you." Andy pulled Leslie closer. "Really...now."

"Watch it!" Leslie quickly kissed Andy's lips, turned and moved closer to the incoming waves. Andy followed. He reached around her waist, pulled Leslie into a tight embrace.

"That was my cousin, so you don't have to worry."

"My rap is so strong that I don't care who you know...nobody in Brooklyn can get close to you. My charm is too cool."

"Oh, really Mr. want-to-be Al Green, Jimmy Walker smooth talkin'..."

"You know my rap is dynamite." Andy moved closer to Leslie.

Their lips touched again, this time lingering. The waves lapped at their feet. Leslie moved away from Andy and stated to walk toward the building. She reached and grabbed Andy's hand. "Come on...follow me back to my office." She guided him from the sandy shore to the cement walkways that led to the first floor office in Building "A".

She opened the door, walked to her desk. Leslie picked up her purse and some papers. This was part of the teaching experience for her Brooklyn College degree. Leslie worked with the Upward Bound program during the fall, spring and a few weeks in the summer. She was finishing up the spring part of her experience.

"Let's catch the subway." Andy opened the front door and followed Leslie out of the building.

They walked toward the subway and caught the BMT back to Leslie's neighborhood. For Andy it reminded him of the morning he went to the draft board. He was full of tension, and some of it lingered and attacked him whenever he got on any BMT train. Now, his overriding emotion was different as he held Leslie's hand.

The train pulled into the station near Leslie's house. The pair walked down the steps onto Broadway near Bushwick Avenue. They passed liquor, bakery, grocery and a pair of five and dime stores. People were mulling around watching the cops on horseback and squad cars cruise up and down Broadway. The people were watching the cops with interest.

Tension from the interaction of cops and crowd created an uneasy truce.

"What's all these people doing near that liquor store,"

Leslie held Andy's hand tighter.

"I don't know, they look menacing."

"Let's get outta here," Leslie said, swallowing hard.

"We'll be alright," Andy reassured her.

Deep down Andy wasn't confident. After all the talk he heard at the barbershop and at City College, any little spark might have caused an incident.

Andy and Leslie picked up the pace, turned at the same time and started to run down Broadway. Out of the corner of his eye, Andy caught sight of the bottle leaving the man's hand, only a few feet from where they stood.

The air was cut by the bottle as it rotated slowly, picking up speed, and as it neared the window of the Broadway Five & Dime store. The bottle crashed into the huge plate glass window shattering it into pieces that flew in every direction. People covered their heads and sprinted from the broken glass and the pursuing cops.

Leslie and Andy ran around the corner, down the street and the two blocks to Leslie's house. They heard the sirens and people yelling on Broadway. Andy's eyes caught a glimpse of Leslie's house. He was thinking about the City College lockout, what he heard downtown and here on Broadway.

There's always been tension, but was it really going to happen? Andy thought of what he saw on the evening news.

Was that about to happen in Brooklyn?

Andy opened the short, black cast iron fence and yanked on Leslie. They ran up the steps and banged on the door. Leslie's mother opened the door and both rushed into the living.

"Mamma!" Leslie reached out and pulled her mother close.

"What is it?" A grimace covered her mother's face.

"Somebody in the crowd threw a bottle at the cops on Broadway and all hell broke loose." Andy tried to tell what happened in as few words as possible. "We got away from there as soon as possible. It wasn't anything big, but I keep hearing things in the streets."

"There...there." Mrs. Groves comforted Leslie. "It'll be alright...you're home now."

Andy said, "I've got to get home, cause if Mamma heard anything about what happened, she'll be worried sick."

"You're leaving?" Leslie released herself from her mother's grip and moved toward Andy. "I'm scared...you know what happened the last time."

"I've got to go." Andy grabbed Leslie and gave her a hug. "I'm going the opposite way...the bus is just a block away. I'll call as soon as I get home."

"Promise."

Andy closed the door, bounded down the steps. He stopped, looked both ways. He turned left down Stewart Street to Gates Avenue. He peered around the corner and saw a bus.

As the bus pulled to the curb, Andy heard sirens and people yelling from around the corner on Broadway. Andy jumped on the bus, deposited his fare, and walked to the middle of the bus where he found a seat. Andy listened as the bus driver described the riot scene.

"Something terrible is going to happen to those crazy fools around the corner." The bus pulled away from the curb and sped down Gates Avenue. "I never thought I'd see something like this. It was tough getting across Broadway. The cops had the intersection blocked.

"It was a war zone. They had people's hands up over their heads against the brick wall with their legs spread-eagle style.

"Man, it reminded me of 'Nam...a war zone."

Chapter Thirty

On Broadway the shattered glass created a carpet that crunched as cops chased rioters from damaged storefronts. The blue, red, and white revolving lights from the tops of police cars created a spectrum of colors that reflected an eerie glow off the broken glass.

Tracy was 5-8 with a 130 pounds covering his frame. His dusky-dark skin blended into the shadows of the room. He peeped from around the desk that used to sit next to the window of the Five & Dime. Tracy saw people running up and down Broadway with stolen TVs, clothes, and toasters.

The bottle he threw was right on the mark. The window broke, and Tracy knew he wanted to be the first into the building. He knew he shouldn't be here, but he couldn't resist stealing something.

Tomorrow, he's have a story to tell to his buddies at lunch at Bushwick High. He'd embellish the story about how he outwitted the cops to get the stolen goods back to his house. Now, he must get out of the building without attracting attention.

Across the street, Tracy saw three cops drag down a looter and beat him until blood spurted from his head. The coast seemed clear for a getaway.

Tracy inched closer to the window, jumping onto the street, crunching glass under his feet when he heard, "Stop!"

Tracy kept running, and then he heard a sound, almost a thud. His legs went from under him. He tripped, with the jeans falling in front, and Tracy landing on the jeans. He couldn't move.

"Call an ambulance."

Tracy looked around to see who was hurt, and then realized he was shot. He couldn't move. His head was resting on the jeans. It was dark and the noises faded.

"What happened?" The sergeant looked at the young black man. The blood was flowing from a wound in his back.

"He wouldn't stop...and I shot him," the cop said as he watched the young man's eyes close.

"This won't go well when people get the news...and in the back. Why didn't you shoot in the air?"

"I don't know...it's been crazy out here...I just panicked."

"Well, it's going to be trouble from now on...Who's over there?"

"That's the all-news station...it'll be all over the city, who knows what will happen now."

This was a guest of inclement wind that would develop into squalls that would blow disastrous riots across Bedford-Stuyvesant and other American inner cities.

Chapter Thirty-one

After getting the Towns eviction notice, Marvs and Golda decided when Andy finished college they would move to Long Island. It was time to get out of Brooklyn. Besides, Golda would be closer to her work and Marvs could always take the Long Island Railroad to a station near his cabstand.

Marvs and Andy planned to spend the day looking at places on Long Island and come back to Queens and watch a New York Mets baseball game at Shea Stadium. Golda didn't want to go to the game, so she decided to spend the day with Sister Love.

The early morning sunshine created a good backdrop as Marvs turned the car from Nostrand Avenue onto Fulton Street. They drove until they found the Long Island Expressway which would take them through Nassau County to Central Islip in Suffolk County.

Going from a concrete dominated environment to one of grass and trees was different. Marvs drove on the Long Island expressway through rolling and sometimes lush green areas of Nassau County. In Suffolk County, there were fewer houses and more trees and grass.

Marvs and Andy passed through sub-divisions and finally found Claremont Road. On the right was the house, a nice split level ranch style home. Marvs and Andy got out of the car and walked to the fence. They stared.

"Mamma would love this...look at the big front yard. There's more green than in our entire block on Gates Avenue."

'Yeah." Marvs smiled.

"How's you pay for this."

"We have good credit and the real estate agent said this was a good neighborhood...black people are welcome."

"I'll help you out, as soon as I get my job."

"I know...we'd better get back before the traffic gets heavy."

"Marvs...don't forget the fresh vegetables for Mamma."

"I won't...The vegetables and the fresh fruits won't wilt in the car while we're at the game."

Marvs and Andy drove to the Long Island Expressway for the hour ride to Queens and the game. After parking the car, they got out.

Marvs and Andy walked through the turnstile into the home of the New York Mets. It had been three years since the Mets moved from the Polo Grounds, in upper Manhattan, to this new facility in Queens. The crowd of people, especially one man with his Walkman turned to the AM radio station carrying Ralph Kiner's play-by-play, swirled around the pair as they moved through the portal and up the stairs to their seats.

The crowd of over 40,000 was going strong with the chant of "Let's Go Mets." It was a big game with the hated Philadelphia Phillies. Marvs and Andy found seats on the third row on the first base side.

"Good seats?" Marvs smiled.

"You can see so much...look there's Cleon Jones!" Andy pointed to the Mets all-star player. Andy looked at the panorama of the field at Shea Stadium. The sunlight created a bright picture-portrait of a vast green playing field where the Big Apple's National League baseball team performed.

Andy leaned forward, a man and a little boy passed behind them to get to their seats, while another fan edged in front. When all the maneuvering was over, Andy looked at his father and sat back in his seat to watch the Mets come from behind and win 4-2 in the bottom of the ninth.

Marvs and Andy walked through the portal and down the ramp. The crowd was in a good mood as they filed out of the stadium and walked across the street to the parking lot .

It was strange seeing Marvs driving anything but a yellow cab, but here he was in the old Plymouth. Andy called it the "putt-putt", because of the sound it made as the engine tried to start as Marvs turned the ignition key.

Marvs drove the car from the parking lot onto Main Street that led away from Shea Stadium. Leaving Queens, the pair headed to Brooklyn. Marvs drove down Broadway, past the gutted buildings from the night before.

"That was a good game." Andy looked to see if he could see Leslie's house as they drove down the street.

"That's why they're called the 'Incredible Mets'." Marvs looked straight ahead as he maneuvered the car down Gates Avenue.

"Thanks." Andy glanced over to his father.

"The tickets were free and I feel that you must take advantage of any freebie," Marvs said, smiling.

"We've got to do this more often." Andy stared at Leslie's house and wondered what she was doing. Marvs' questioning got his attention as he turned toward his father.

"If you get that newspaper job in DC or Baltimore, then you won't be close…but wherever life takes you, we'll always be with you.

"I hope we can make it through this spring and summer. After what I saw the other night, I think things can explode at any time. You be careful, 'cause I feel something can happen anytime, I hear things as I drive around the city. I'm stocking up food and other things in case we get involved in something big…"

"Something?" Andy looked puzzled.

What you've seen on TV in some of the other cities may come to Bed-Sty…that's the feeling I get."

Andy looked out of the window as the car crossed Marcy Avenue and into the four hundred block of Gates Avenue. Marvs parallel parked in front of the Brownstone, and Andy grabbed the bags containing the fresh fruit and vegetables. When they opened the door they found an agitated Golda waiting.

She rushed through the open door and grabbed Marvs.

"What?" Marvs looked puzzled.

"I'm glad you're back," Golda said sobbing.

"Tell me what!"

"Somebody got him."

"Got who?"

"Jesse Towns!"

"What...Again!"

"He was in his office a couple of hours ago when we heard all the commotion. Sister Love, Trina and I came out of our doors at the same time. It was a gunshot!"

"Oh my God." Marvs pulled away from his wife.

"Yeah...we saw Randall running up the steps with a gun in his hand. He ran by us and into his room. We continued down the steps to the basement. There he was."

"Who?"

"Jesse Towns was lying on the floor, staring at the ceiling with blood pouring out of his chest...he's in intensive care at Kings county Hospital."

Marvs stepped back, looked at Golda and then at Andy.

Chapter Thirty-two

The Antioch Baptist Church reminded first-time visitors of a medieval cathedral in England rather than a gospel church on Chauncey Avenue near Fulton Street Brooklyn. Two arches soared into the overcast night sky that kept the moon hid for most of the evening. The bright neon sign showed the name of following announcements, "Gospel Night, 8 P.M."

Marvs' group was on the program, near the end, to sing their version of "How Great Thou Art." Coming so near the end of the program meant the group was well thought of, especially since they were close to the evening's headliners.

Reds, Walker, Thurmond and Marvs sat in a little room off the main sanctuary and waited for their turn to perform on one of the most famous pulpits in Brooklyn. The group was sixth on the list of nine to perform. The conversation turned from performing to the shooting in Marvs' Brownstone.

"I heard about the shooting on the news." Reds adjusted his tie.

"That was scary for Golda...to walk in and see a man on the basement floor with a hole in his chest, lying in a pool of blood." Marvs turned his head and looked at the picture of Christ on the wall.

"That man was a scoundrel and a thief," Reds said. "I knew him from the neighborhood. He never had anything and stole the Brownstone y'all are living in.

Remember, when they found a woman murdered in the trunk of a car near Brighton Beach a few years ago, that was his wife. The cops never found who shot her, but the word on the streets was that Towns either did it or had James Randall kill her, 'cause you know they were into a lot of illegal things together. I'm not sorry for anything that has happened to him."

Marvs moved across the room and faced Reds.

"It's just too bad it had to happen in our building...James Randall has been arrested for attempted murder. I knew something was up between those two, but I never suspected it to reach that level."

Thurmond stretched. "When we go on?"

"We got a while." Reds moved to the window that looked out onto Chauncey Avenue and watched the late comers.

While Marvs' group waited to perform before the religious crowd at Antioch, down at Barbara's Lounge on Fulton Street, Mother Nature and Sweet Thang were getting the bar into the groove to "Party". When they walked into the bar, something was going on in the back alley.

Mother Nature ordered a scotch on the rocks and seated him at the bar and then went to the back. One of the night fighters, the name given to women who frequented bars and were always in the middle of many bar altercations, told her man to get ready to go home.

The man was 5-8 and 145 pounds of drunken arrogance.

Big Elisha was 300 pounds of angry woman.

"I ain't going nowhere woman until I'm good and ready."

He walked away with a smirk on his face. He felt something close in on him, but it was too late.

Big Elisha grabbed him and flipped him, head first, into a dumpster. All you could see was his feet kicking in the air. Mother Nature was laughing so hard, she almost tripped over the door seal. When she reached the bar where Sweet Thang was enjoying his drink, she couldn't tell the story for laughing so hard.

"What's wrong with you?" Sweet Thang put his drink down.

"Big Elisha just flipped her man into the dumpster with just one swoop..."

"She what?" Sweet Thang swallowed his drink in one gulp.

"You heard me, she grabbed that little man and threw him head first into the garbage can."

Everybody around Sweet Thang and Mother Nature ran to the back alley to catch a glimpse. The patrons stopped shooting pool and dancing to the music of Booker T and the MGs' "Green Onions". The melodic Memphis sound was an instrumental melody with a beat that made the good foot even better.

Everybody looked on while Big Elisha hauled her man by the collar through the bar. As she released him someone yelled from near the jukebox. "Bet you'll carry your boney butt home now."

He got up, dusted the trash from his clothes. He never said a word. He walked, trying to keep some dignity.

"Now you ready, honey?" Big Elisha walked behind him. Barbara's lounge was jumping with people laughing, drinking and talking about what Big Elisha did.

It was getting close to time for Marvs' group to perform. The Master of Ceremony came and told the group to get ready. The Quartet put on their tuxedo coats and walked to the sanctuary. Some people said the group was like the Soul Stirrers.

On stage the group lined up with Marvs, Walker, Reds, and Thurmond. They looked sharp. The sweat rolled off their faces as the lights heated up the pulpit area. Walker, the lead singer, started, followed by Marvs the alto, Reds the bass, and Thurmond the tenor. "When Christ shall come...take me home...When I shall bow...How Great Thou Art..."

The sanctuary was filled with 'amens'. The group's electric rendition of the hymn created quite a stir in the gospel audience. The 'amens' and clapping brought them on again for another chorus of the hymn.

Back in the room, the group changed clothes and congratulated each other and set the next practice date.

"Can we still meet at your apartment?"

"All that business with the courts and Towns' shooting won't change our practicing." Marvs finished dressing.

Everybody grabbed their stuff and started out the door.

"Let me know what's going on," Reds said.

"I will." Marvs walked into the sanctuary and saw Golda and Andy. They gave him a big hug. They walked out into the cool spring air. The street was dark as the church lights and the neon sigh were both dark.

"You sang well and looked even better." Golda squeezed Marvs' hand.

"Good job…Mr. Marvs." Then he got into the back seat of the Plymouth.

"Thanks." Marvs turned to Andy. "You and Leslie going to the street festival in Harlem tomorrow?"

"You bet."

"Be careful." Golda turned, a concerned look across her face.

"Why didn't I know that was coming?" Andy said, smiling.

Marvs drove from Chauncey to Fulton street. They headed to the Fulton street diner to get some soul food.

"There's Barbara's lounge." Andy pointed.

"You know Mother Nature and Sweet Thang must be partying down." Marvs laughed.

"Sweet Thang is probably so drunk he doesn't know where he's standing." Golda put her head in her hands for a minute and looked straight inside Barbara's lounge. Sweet Thang was feeling that good buzz when he had a few scotches on the rocks. Mother Nature knew she had to drive home or they'd be headed for the 57th Precinct.

"Sweet Thang." Mother Nature walked toward the bar, "It's time to go.'

"Really."

"Yeah really."

"Suppose I don't want to go?"

"Suppose you end up in a dumpster?'

"Good point." Sweet Thang smiled, downed the scotch and headed for the door. "Wrong way." Mother Nature pointed toward the front door.

"Give me the keys and get in." She knew it was not good for him to drink. One day he'd have to face those Vietnam demons without alcohol as a backup. Mother Nature knew some changes must come because Sweet Thang was killing himself.

Chapter Thirty-three

From the Harlem Renaissance in the thirties to Adam Clayton Powell's new African-American village, the small strip of upper Manhattan was where black America's heart beat.

The Apollo theater, along 125th street, had witnessed some of the greatest black entertainers from Cab Calloway to Al Green. The Beat goes on.

Now, the bright sunlight created images of light and dark shadowy people bouncing off buildings.

Andy and Leslie bounded up the subway steps from the tunnel where the "A" train, made famous by Duke Ellington and his classic musical composition, make its 125th street stop.

They exited the tunnel holding hands. The wind gusted along 125th street creating a breezy atmosphere for the annual street festival.

Andy gazed down the crowded street looking for any familiar faces from City College. Leslie's Brooklyn College classmates would be scarce in the crowd since few people from Brooklyn traveled up to Harlem.

African garments dominated, the blues like the sky, reds the colors of tomatoes and oranges like the juicy fruits from Florida, plus the patterns mixed from various colors that sparkled and attracted the eye's attention.

The vendors' booths stretched on both sides along 125th street from Eighth Avenue to Madison Avenue. Police barricades kept the area free of cars so people could maneuver from sidewalks to create a mobile people walk.

Andy looked down an alley and saw a junkie. He was bobbing and weaving coming onto 125th street. Andy swallowed hard. He concentrated harder to get the image out of his brain. Andy's gaze moved from the junkie to Leslie.

Andy and Leslie had planned this outing for the past two

years. It was a mini-vacation getaway from their everyday routine. A chance to explore something new together. A chance to learn something new about their culture and what it would take to develop a life together.

Andy stopped in mid-stride when a bookstall caught his eye. For two years he had wanted a copy of that book, but in the department stores and at City College, it was too expensive. Now, there it was, with the white cover and words "Soul on Ice" dominating the front jacket.

Everybody at City was reading Eldridge Cleaver's book, which was helping fuel the revolution of the young black American mind. A mind that was blank and needed a mold to put into form changes in an atmosphere of increased black consciousness. Now, it was time to change, forming new ideas of love, respect for the race, and all people of color in the world.

Andy stared while Leslie yanked on his arm. He pulled her back to him. Andy pushed Leslie towards the stall and then put her hand on the book. "Pick it up."

Leslie felt the cover of the book with the letters of Soul in red and Ice in blue. "That's it."

"What?" Leslie handed the book to Andy.

"Finally."

Andy grabbed the book and flipped through the pages. He handed the vendor five dollars. It was ten dollars at the City College bookstore. "Now, I can read one of the books that's getting black people to think."

"Really...let's see some more stuff before you start the revolution." Leslie pulled Andy away from the stall. "I want to enjoy being with my man before I lose him to some war in some urban battleground..."

People quick-stepped to avoid bumping into each other. Andy missed stepping on the toes of a man in a dashiki. "I hope it doesn't come to that, but you never know... I could be another H. Rap Brown."

"Sure, Andy, and your mother would have your black butt

in a sling. Your revolution better end with a degree from City College."

"I know, but the struggle is coming, and it will catch us before we know it..."

"Andy." Leslie reached, turned Andy's head toward a crowd of people across the street where a speaker was memorizing the listeners.

"...racial, economic injustice must..." There he was, H. Rap Brown.

Andy looked, listened, and pulled Leslie away from the crowd, which sprinkled applause at key moments in the speech. Occasionally you heard a, 'Right On Brother.'"

Andy hurried with Leslie following him. "They look angry, lets find another place near Madison and 125th. I don't feel comfortable around some of those militants. I recognize some of them from the lockout at City College. They mean business."

Andy was facing backwards and nodding his head in the direction of a dark-complexioned brother with the greenish-gold skullcap. "See that guy in the black shirt, he never smiles...I know he's bad news."

Andy and Leslie walked to a booth a few feet from the rally to get a hot dog with mustard and relish and some fresh-fried chicken. The lady pulled the chicken out of the hot, splattering grease and put it on a paper towel. Next came the fries and some fried sweet potatoes. She put all this on two plates. Andy paid for the two orders and soda pops.

The lady, with her grease-splattered apron, smiled. "You're a nice couple." She handed the change to Andy, who slipped it in his front pocket, and then gave the plates to Leslie. They walked to an area with some empty benches to enjoy their food. Some people moved in pairs, but most in groups. When they finished eating. Andy grabbed the paper plates and put them in the nearest garbage can. They walked down 125th street toward The Apollo, away from Madison Avenue in the direction of Eighth Avenue, toward the subway.

"Andy," she said. He looked in Leslie's direction. "Are you thinking about getting involved in the movement?"

Andy turned away.

"Look at me...know you're thinking about it. I can feel this anger building and it will come out some way. Don't answer me right now, but remember that anger is dangerous and once its unleashed, it will take you to levels of violence that you might regret...don't make a rash decision, but think about the consequences for you, I mean your future...our future.

"I saw your eyes the other night when the cops were beating people in the crowd on Broadway. I never saw that expression before...that's not you. We change things, but not with a quick fix called violence. If there is violence, it will hurt us in the long run. Keep your back straight and the only weapon you need is words. They can be effective. Remember what Dr. King tells us that 'nobody can ride your back when it's straight.'"

Andy stared at Leslie.

He knew she was telling the truth, but he felt ineffective. She was reading his thoughts. He threw the empty soda containers in the trash basket. It was like throwing away a few negative ideas.

Andy reached and touched Leslie's hand. He squeezed.

"Andy?"

"Yeah."

"I love you."

"I love you back."

Andy squeezed her hand a second time and with the other he clutched the copy of "Soul on Ice." Two forces were pulling at the very inner-core of his being.

Andy looked across the street from the Apollo at the "Black Panthers" rally. Andy and Leslie walked under The Apollo Marquee advertising tomorrow night's soul review— Al Green and some Motown group called The Supremes. The pair walked toward the subway and the "A" train to

Brooklyn.

"Thanks." Andy bounded down the steps with Leslie behind him.

"For what?"

"For being my conscience."

Andy kissed Leslie. They walked through the turnstile, holding hands.

Chapter Thirty-four

Andy tossed in his sleep. He thought about Leslie's smile and flashing brown eyes. He rolled over and looked at the clock, midnight. This night he had flashbacks about the time he was about to get drafted. He had cold sweats then and now.

"Yes 'em."

"What's that noise?" Andy couldn't figure out what was happening. He walked to the window facing Gates Avenue. He blinked, wiped the sleep from his eyes, and then moved closer to the window, with his nose touching the glass.

"Oh my God!" Andy jerked his face away from the window, tripping over his own feet and failing on the floor.

Chapter Thirty-five

1:00 a.m.

The windows in the apartment buildings along Gates Avenue were filled with residents. The smile-less faces and blink-less eyes reflected the flames that were eating at various businesses along the avenue.

Bricks slammed through plate glass windows. People's feet crunched the broken glass as they stepped through the open spaces in front of the buildings. The crowd surged up and down the street in a mindless attack on businesses, especially those of white owners. They carried portable TVs, stereos, cans of food and anything that could be carried in their arms.

The riot erupted on Gates Avenue about the same time that it hit Fulton Street, Atlantic Avenue, Broadway and other areas, the same volcanic emotional tide of violence that rocked the inner cities of Brooklyn, Harlem, Detroit, Chicago and Watts in Los Angeles.

Andy watched the surreal revolution below his window. Rioters ripped through Gates Avenue. From his vantage point he saw a man trip, followed by aTV soaring up into the air until it couldn't go any higher and then it fell back to the concrete sidewalk where it crashed. With a loudthud many pieces scattered over the pavement. That wasn't the only disaster he witnessed, as a carton of frozen fish was dropped, went tumbling across the concrete and finally rested under a car.

People looting.

People jumping out of burning cars.

People bumping into each other carrying stolen goods.

Andy looked straight into the distance and saw flames leaping into the air from buildings on Fulton Street. There was wreckage everywhere: the riot was not stopping, but expanding with pillaging, looting and burning!

Tears formed in Andy's eyes.

Some buildings were gutted with the iron-protective grates learning on the concrete sidewalk.

Flames leaped from burning cars that lined the street.

Smoke rose from the buildings.

Sirens blared in the streets.

Chapter Thirty-six

3:00 a.m.

Andy pulled the shade down and stepped back from the window. Images flashed through the eggshell-colored curtains. He flopped back in the bed and stared straight ahead. He couldn't believe what was occurring on Gates Avenue.

For years Andy had heard, but didn't really listen to all the rhetoric about Black America being in a state of war: self-determination, cultural, and economic freedom. That the police was the military arm of the establishment.

The combination of two words — Black and Power — scared America! And now the rioting would be the catalyst for a backlash against the national Black community.

Andy leaned back on the bed and closed his eyes. He flinched when he heard something crash on the pavement. Most of the businesses on Gates Avenue were white owned.

The community felt the police were there to protect the outside owners, not for the community.

Now, everything was out of control.

"Andy."

Golda and Marvs came into his room. "We were watching out of the living room window…"

"It's terrible."

Marvs moved to the window and peeped out from behind the curtains. Golda sat next to Andy.

"Get back, Marvs…somebody might shoot."

"I'm okay." Marvs looked toward the corner. "I'm glad the car is in the shop. Look at all the cars burning in the street." Marvs let the shade close back over the window. He sat at Andy's desk.

"Is everybody okay in the building?" Andy reached over and hugged his mother.

"Yeah, I called everybody. Thank God the telephones are still working. We locked the doors, especially those on the first floor, down in the basement and out back. Trina and Sister Love said everybody next door is okay. John Randall is still in jail because he's the chief suspect in Town's shooting..."

"What are we going to do?" Andy looked at his father.

Boom!

The sound startled Golda, who grabbed Andy's hand. Marvs moved to the window.

"No!" Golda yelled.

Marvs, after taking a quick peek, moved quickly. "A car blew up near the corner."

"Why Lord?" Golda moved toward her husband.

Chapter Thirty-seven

5:00 a.m.

On the early morning news, the riot stories bounced off the TV screen like the bullets bounced off the buildings in Brooklyn.

Bedford-Stuyvesant, Brooklyn was now under Martial law.

The mayor had made that decision so that the National Guard could assist local police. Things were out of control

The TV set was the center of attention for the Pilgrim family. The camera focused on burning buildings, the looting and the death of people in the faceless crowd.

On television, Detroit, Watts in Los Angeles, Harlem and Bedford-Stuyvesant were in flames. What was the cause? So many things, plus the death of Martin Luther King added the fuel to the tinderbox of emotions.

Andy, Golda, and Marvs saw reality out the window and the surreal on the television.

"Is this really happening?" Golda looked at Marvs. "Why?"

"It's been coming a long time. Little things built up into larger things."

"People get tired of put downs," Andy said. "What they're doing is wrong, wrong...people shouldn't loot, rob, steal, or destroy. It goes against everything we believe.

"I thought about joining the Black Panthers and being part of the radical change, but I realized that wasn't for me."

Marvs moved to the window and raised the shades on a chaotic street scene with smoldering cars and gutted buildings.

"That's not life...that's the death of our people. If we continue on this path of violence, it will be met by violence.

"Guess who will be the loser?

"What our leaders say is right, and I don't just mean what

Martin Luther King said, but Malcolm X, Stokely Carmichael, and the rest are right, but it must be done in peace...not like this." Marvs pointed to the chaotic scene of destruction on the street. He pulled the curtains back and walked toward Golda.

They hugged.

Andy looked at his parents.

Chapter Thirty-eight

8 a.m.

Andy jumped up from the bed as if from a bad dream. He walked across the room to the window and pulled the shade. He looked. It was surreal, a wasteland of destruction. Cars burned, protective iron gates torn away from buildings covered the front of many businesses: A war zone.

The most sinister feeling was created when Andy saw city policemen and National Guardsmen patrolling Gates Avenue.

Nobody was walking, just like in a war zone, the curfew was in effect until the next day. That meant nobody could leave their apartment.

The dream was a reality. There had been a riot, which brought out grief and fear on Gates Avenue. The violence people saw in Saigon was now the violence of Brooklyn.

A knock at the door startled the Pilgrim household. Marvs, Golda, and Andy met at the living room door, which opened to the hallway.

"Who's There?" Marvs moved closer to the door.

"Open…it's me, Sister Love."

Marvs pushed the deadbolt lock back, then unlocked the two other locks. "It's bad out there." Sister Love rushed into the living room and closed the door behind her. "Mother Nature called and said Fulton Street was a disaster. Sweet Thang said it reminded him of Vietnam. She said he's drinking heavier than ever…"

Golda sat down on the couch with Marvs. Sister Love moved to the doorway, while Andy stood in the doorway leading to his bedroom.

Marvs took a step, turned the knob on the combination stereo and television. "I was going to put on the television to see what's going in other cities…we're still under Martial law, the man on the radio said about an hour ago. "

Andy crossed the living room and headed to the kitchen.

"Nothing takes that boy's appetite." Golda smiled. It was a normal everyday moment. Andy returned the smile and kept walking toward the refrigerator in the kitchen.

"So many people hurt for no reason." Marvs found the channel.

"Where are we going to get food?" Golda looked in the kitchen at Andy making his favorite peanut butter and jelly sandwich and a big glass of orange juice to wash it down.

"At least the lights are on." Sister Love looked at Andy and shook her head. "That sandwich is too thick for me."

"That's the way I like it," Andy said, munching on the sandwich and washing it down with juice. "I talked to some of my friends in Harlem and they said around 125th Street and even Amsterdam Avenue, it's bad like here on Gates Avenue...cops and National Guardsmen everywhere."

When Marvs found the channel everybody quieted. The riots had erupted in over 20 American cities including Bedford-Stuyvesant in Brooklyn, Harlem in Manhattan, Watts in Los Angeles, inner cities of Detroit and Chicago. The home of Martin Luther King, Atlanta, was quiet. Because of all these disruptions people's lives changed. The worst riots in modern American history erupted across the land of the free.

The eyes of people reflected a change in beliefs. The chains that bind are invisible when crime is rising and rent is past due in a crumbling-down building , where more and more people ditch reality with drugs. We shall overcome by any means. There was enough blame for everybody. The mainstream sixties viewpoint of destroying the progressive viewpoint was as much at fault as the violent reaction of the inner cities.

The church burning in the south, the killing of Martin Luther Kind preventing the rise of a black messiah which prevented meaningful steps for individual freedom.

Marvs reached over and turned the television off as the camera showed the fire eating at buildings and turning them into ash. "I've seen and heard enough."

"What about us?" Golda asked. "How long will we have to stay locked up like caged animals?"

"Until it's safe to go outside." Marvs hugged Golda.

"We'll know something soon." Andy took the last bite of his peanut butter and jelly sandwich. He gulped the orange juice. He smacked his lips. "Believe me...they'll stop this things before they have tanks rumbling down Broadway in Manhattan."

"As long as it's in the ghettos...nobody cares." Marvs stared at the photo of Martin Luther King. "I'm sad you've got to make your way in a world filled with backlash...where idealism has ended.

"I'm so afraid that repression is in the air and just living will be more difficult for you in the future. When those buildings went up in flames it was just more that ash from the burning buildings that went up into smoke... There were lives and futures of people in this area."

Marvs lowered his head and grabbed his face with his hands. Andy went into his bedroom. He'd worried about Leslie and now it was time to call her. Leslie was slow answering her phone, but finally she picked up.

"Hello Andy."

"How'd you know it was me?"

"I figured you'd be calling about this time."

"You know me?"

"You'd better believe it."

"Is it bad up your way?"

"Broadway is gutted...my brother, Ralph, walked in from work as the riot hit."

"I miss you...I love you."

"I love you, too."

"Remember when we were at the Harlem street festival and I told you I wanted to join the revolution?"

"Yeah."

"Well...I'm glad you talked with me. I could've been out

there in the middle of the riots. I feel there must be another way..."

"I've been scared for three days and you could've been out there in all that chaos, but I'm glad you're safe. I love you Andy."

"Leslie...I love you so much."

"And I love you back."

Chapter Thirty-nine

The pilgrims and the other residents of the Brownstone stayed in their apartments and homes for three days before the curfew was lifted. Andy heard news on the all-news station. He hadn't seen any National Guardsmen or police walking along Gates in the last twenty-four hours. Now, with this news, it was good enough time for Andy to venture out and see the damage.

Andy knew Golda wouldn't like the idea, but his father would probably be on his side. In a few hours he'd tell his parents he wanted to go and see conditions outside.

Andy knocked on the door of his parent's room. Marvs looked up.

"Andy?" Golda answered.

"Yes 'em."

"Come in."

"You want to go out?"

"How'd you know?" Andy looked at his mother.

"I heard you talkin' on the phone."

"Well."

"I talked it over with your father before you even walked into the room and we decided that we wouldn't oppose you, but we'll be worried until you get back."

"If I see anything wrong, I'll get back quick.

I've got to see. I've got to find out what is happening."

"Andy, I know."

Andy walked across the room to where Golda was sitting on the couch. He leaned over and kissed his mother on the forehead and whispered, "I'll be all right."

Golda grabbed his hand and squeezed hard, before letting it go. Andy didn't look back as he closed and locked the door to the apartment. He walked down the stairs passing Sister Love's door. He saw it opened slowly.

"Andy Michael Pilgrim, you be careful." Sister Love closed the door just as quickly. Andy smiled and kept walking to the front door. He breathed deeply.

Andy reached for the doorknob, turned it, opened the front door and was confronted with many odors, but the odor of burning wood dominated the scents coming into his nostrils. In his apartment, Andy had watched the devastation through a glass window, like on a television screen, but now the reality of the smells and sights gave him a new prospective on what was left of Gates Avenue.

His eyes soared up toward the blue sky and then his gaze slowly descended toward the tops of buildings. Everything was normal. Lowering his focus his sight finally rested on the street.

What attacked his vision and destroyed his past remembrances was the sight of gutted, fire-eaten buildings turned to grayish ash. He realized how fortunate his family had been since the majority of damage was across the street, not on the 423 side of the block. Amid all the devastation of the Key Food grocery was a can of tomato soup, it's red and white covering rolling in the gutter.

"Morning, Andy."

Andy nodded and kept walking. The scene seemed normal, yet something was wrong.

Andy was numb.

He walked past the barbershop, which was still intact, but the looted fish market was in ruins. The cash register was splattered on the sidewalk with the change drawer opened and empty. The glass counter, which contained the crushed ice to keep the fish fresh, was shattered and pieces of glass littered the sidewalk in front of the store. Andy gazed.

He moved forward, stepping on the broken pieces of glass. He kicked one large piece from under his feet. He kept walking down Gates Avenue, passing the results of the riots and the chaos, which had devastated Bedford-Stuyvesant for two days.

Andy knew people who owned these stores wouldn't take this and would be the backbone of a backlash that would attack his inner-city neighborhood. Their world, filled with acrid backlash, would be different from the world he knew. Idealism was over and repression would be in the air, cruel repression like what thwarted the marchers in the south.

Andy thought about Stokely Carmichael's rhetoric that united the black youth. He knew that mainstream America's sixties viewpoint of destroying the progressive movement had been given a big stick to whip the minorities. It was also to prevent the rise of a black messiah. Now, it was about to happen.

As he walked down Gates Avenue, he passed Mr. Possum's candy store, which was standing, because of selective targeting, but the dry cleaners was completely gutted with clothes all over the sidewalk. He wondered if any of his family's clothes were in the cleaners. He remembered getting everything Tuesday before the riots.

Andy turned the corner onto Nostrand Avenue and found damages just as bad as Gates Avenue. Andy ran down the block to the Methodist Church. It was Okay. He felt better. He continued toward Lafayette Avenue. It was the same scenario. Minority businesses were not damaged, but anything owned by people outside the community was looted. Right or wrong didn't matter. Just seek and destroy and not worry about the consequences. Eldridge Cleaver wanted the brothers to take meaningful steps toward individual freedom. Was this freedom? Destroy and then ask questions later. Andy peered down Nostrand Avenue and saw the same thing. He saw enough. It was time to head back to his apartment. He turned away from Lafayette and walked at a brisk pace. It was time to wake up out of his nightmare.

Andy reached home, bounded up the steps and didn't look back, because something might be reaching up to pull him back into the nightmare on the streets. He turned the key, opened and closed the door. He leaned back against the door.

He closed his eyes for an instant, then opened his eyes and looked at the four flights of steps and bounded them in three leaps.

Before he could open the door, Golda was opening it for him. She reached and hugged him. Marvs walked behind them and pat Andy on the Back.

"Well?"

Andy pulled himself away from Golda. He put his arms around his mother and walked her to the couch. The television was on, news anchors talking about the riots. Marvs turned the sound down.

"It'll never be the same," Andy said. "The white-owned stores have been destroyed and the Black-owned businesses have been left standing. People are not going to take this lying down. There's going to be a backlash."

"I figured as much," Marvs said.

"It's scary, "Andy said. "The only thing I can compare it to was what Sweet Thang described about the devastation in Vietnam…"

"Not like we knew it," Andy said. "Something new is coming. If we don't do it ourselves, people will come in and do things for us. Everything is different out there…I saw things I never saw before in my life."

"Can we survive?" Marvs asked.

"Yeah…but things will be different for us."

"How?" Golda looked at Marvs and then at Andy.

Andy shrugged his shoulders.

Chapter Forty

Andy fought with his pillow. The night wouldn't let him go. It was worse than the night before he was going to the draft board. What he saw during the afternoon revisited him in his dreams. He didn't have control over his nightmares.

He jumped out of bed, walked to the window and sat on the sill. He hadn't had any cravings for dope. Nothing. When Peter saw Andy, he would point to his arm and laugh. Peter mouthed the word heroine.

The first rays of the sun bounced off buildings across from the Brownstone. The light beams filtered through the broken glass hanging in the devastated areas of the building creating multi-colored images on broken furniture and burned clothes.

Andy stared. The sunlight made the darkness retreat and images became clear. Two weeks had passed since the riots. Some people repaired their buildings, while other businesses remained shuttered and closed. Andy looked and then walked back to his bed. He settled in his favorite spot.

Andy reached toward a table, turned the knob of the radio to WBLS so he could hear the latest news and music. Lenny Welch came on with "Since I Fell For You". He enticed you with his deep soulful voice when he started singing, "When you just give love, and never get love, you 'd better let love depart..."

Andy laid back and his mind drifted with the song, swaying with every beat as the sunlight danced across his face. Andy moved closer to the wall without opening his eyes. His mind drifted and finally fell into a deep sleep. He tossed and turned. Andy rolled in the bed, almost falling over the edge.

Andy's foot touched the floor and he pushed himself back onto the bed. On the first ring, the phone startled him, and then the second ring made him realize that it was the telephone. On the third ring, Andy reached toward the table and in one movement turned the radio off and picked up the telephone receiver and brought it to his ear.

"Hello...hi baby...what time is it?" Andy smiled when he heard Leslie's voice.

"Thinking about you." Leslie answered. "What took you so long to get the phone?"

"I was sleeping...what time is it?"

"7:30 in the morning, and you should've been out of the house and ready for your class."

"Yeah, I know...I'll make up all that work."

"What's up?"

"Andy...I've got something to tell you and it's going to be tough."

"Speak."

"I hate when you say that." Leslie played at being annoyed.

"Sorry."

"Well...my parents," Leslie hesitated, "They told me that...that...that, because of the riots and chaos over the last two weeks it's no longer safe for me to see you."

Andy pulled the phone away from his ear and started to lay it back on its base.

"Andy!...Andy!...Andy!" Leslie screamed into the phone.

Gradually, Andy put the phone back to his ear.

"Leslie, I don't believe you. What have the riots got to do with our relationship?"

"My parents don't want me to come into that part of town..."

"It's not me that was part of the riots...Leslie, you know the real reason for this."

"You don't believe that, Andy?"

"Yes I do...my skin isn't light enough, my father is a cab driver, I won't graduate from Columbia and we don't live in a fine neighborhood like Flatbush."

"Andy!"

"Don't Andy...!"

"Andy Michael Pilgrim calm down and let me finish telling you how I feel. May I finish please?...Don't you dare speak or I will hang up on you and never talk to you again."

"Sp...oh all right, tell me."

"Nothing will ever separate you from me. I respect and love my parents, but I will still see you. They didn't like it, but I told them how I felt and they have to learn to deal with that because you're my life and the person I'm going to spend the rest of my life with. I don't want to go behind my parents' back, but I will because I love you Andy Michael Pilgrim. Andy...if you don't know that by now you're crazy.

"I told you what they said because I felt that there should be nothing that can separate us or that we couldn't talk about. I feel we must do three things for our relationship to grow and that is respect each other, trust each other, and communicate with each other..."

"Leslie," Andy said softly.

"Yes, Andy."

"I love you."

"I know...but most of all I wanted you to know and realize you don't have anything to worry about."

"I don't want to lose you."

"You won't."

"When can we meet?"

"Andy...just call and we'll find the place."

"I will."

"When?"

"Late this afternoon when I get back from City College."

"Love me."

"Leslie, jewels and stars can't match your beauty...An angel-looking princess who is you...Nobody else can be as beautiful as you, every kind of beauty there is, I see in you. Ten times more beautiful than anyone else. If beauty were in riches, you'd be full of wealth."

"Andy I didn't know you were a poet."

"You bring out so many things I didn't know I could do or say or create...I guess its love."

"That's the truth."

"Love you."

"Love you back...I'll call you later." Andy put the receiver back on its base. He closed his eyes and let his head ease back on the pillow.

Chapter Forty-one

Andy opened the outside door and saw the mailman walking down the street. He decided to see if he'd get any letters before leaving for his afternoon class.

He watched the mailman put some letters into each mailbox, located inside the doorway to each apartment building. When he got to 423 he handed Andy the Pilgrims' mail, put the rest into each tenant's box.

Andy shuffled the various. He found the one with the Vietnam postmark. It was from Tony Yang. Andy raced up the steps to his apartment. He closed the door and tore the side of envelope and pulled out the letter.

He turned the knob on the radio, found WBLS, sat back to read his letter from the war zone. That place would've been his home if had passed the military's physical exam. Andy read about how the rainstorms came on a regular basis and the heat was unbearable. Sometimes the stench from unwashed bodies would pull down like a weighted exercise bar.

His friend told him about the underground radio station where he could get the latest music the American government didn't want them to hear. He loved the latest, a Jimmy Hendrix tune.

Soldiers could rarely call home, so communication was done through letters. They gave a glimpse of life on the battlefront. Tony said he was on the bunk in his barracks when he wrote Andy.

He opened the letter with "Yo bro." Tony said he didn't know how to continue, but he had to finish telling his buddy the details. Tony said he cried while writing the letter. The tears dripped on the paper. He was fortunate, writing with a ballpoint pen, so the tears didn't create inkblots on the page.

Andy read Tony's words. He became depressed.

"Yesterday, Jose Morales was the front man as "B" company was on patrol. We were tracking Viet Cong, who had thrown some bombs at us, when I heard a scream. The sound numbered my senses...but when I got to the front of the column everybody was surrounding what was left of him. He had stepped on a landmine and it blew off the lower half of his body. Parts of Jose littered the jungle floor.

"I fell on my knees and grabbed his hand and with the others wiped his bloody face. I heard myself scream 'Oh God, not Jose!' I beat the ground. I was furious. I jumped up and started shooting in the surrounding jungle before some of the other soldiers grabbed me and pulled me to the ground."

Andy put the letter on the bed, reached up and massaged his forehead. The ache intensified. He realized it could have been him in the jungle. Now, this was added to the stress from the riots and it was taking its toll.

The phone rang and Andy was deep in thought. It kept ringing for a while when he finally picked up the receiver. "Yes."

"Andy?" Leslie's soft voice came through the phone.

"Yeah."

"I thought you were at City College, I didn't expect you to be at home."

"I was going when I saw the postman and decided to see if there was any mail for us before leaving to catch the subway. There was a letter from my friend Tony Yang."

"What did he have to say?"

"Nothing really Leslie, jus' that Jose Morales was killed!" he snapped. Andy's sharp reply startled and angered Leslie.

"You don't have to take it out on me."

"Well, you don't have to worry about me anymore."

"I won't." Leslie hung up the phone.

Andy cried as he rolled over onto his stomach.

The knock at the door announced that his mother was at the door waiting to speak to him.

"Andy."

"Yes 'em."

"What's wrong?"

"Nothing, just…just everybody get out of my life?"

"Andy."

Andy jumped off the bed, running by his mother. "I'm sorry, but I've got to get outta here for a while."

"Where you going?"

"Out." Andy walked toward the door and bounded down the stairs.

"Andy! Andy!" Golda ran out the apartment door and yelled down the staircase, but Andy was out the front door and down the street, running toward Nostrand Avenue.

Andy heard his mother calling, but didn't answer. He ran down the street with his thoughts out-racing feet. The people who loved him the most he was pushing away. He argued with his father last night, then Leslie and finally his mother. The world was crowding him and he didn't know how to react. The riots, his best friend fighting for his life in Vietnam, the possibility of being a dope addict, the thought of not graduating, which was the main reason for not going to Vietnam in the first place, was eating his inner soul alive.

His thoughts crashed in all corners of his brain and then he exploded.

"Why don't people leave me alone. I can't be everything to everybody," he yelled back so his mother could hear him.

Andy stopped running and sat down on a stoop right before he got to Fulton Street. He put his face in his hands and cried. He spoke out loud, "Leave me alone, I'm not perfect and stop trying to make me."

Andy didn't notice the familiar figure walking in his direction. He didn't hear the man yelling at him. Only when he heard, "Boy, what you dong sitting on them steps?" did Andy look up to see Sweet Thang smiling at him.

Chapter Forty-two

Andy covered his face with his palms. He moved his face upward, separating the palms so he could smell Sweet Thang's bourbon breath blow in his face. He wanted to turn and run, but couldn't. He started straight ahead.

"Andy." Sweet Thang stepped back.

Andy leaned back, almost falling backwards onto the cement steps.

"Boy...what you doing here?"

Sweet Thang sat down...tears surged out of Andy's eyes and rolled down his cheeks.

"My best friend Jose died," Andy blurted.

"Where?"

"Somewhere near Da Nang, I was reading this letter, my eyes started to water, I got full and couldn't take my parents pressuring me. The riots. Leslie's attitude and my friend's death were too much." Andy was in a mood to make some life-altering decisions, like quitting City College, quit Leslie forever or maybe even move away from Brooklyn. "I ran out of the house. I didn't care...and there is one more thing. I haven't told anybody, but the night Peter and his friends beat me up, he shot heroine in my arm. I haven't felt any cravings, only...I'm scared."

"Get up!" Sweet Thang jumped to his feet pulling Andy with him.

"Where we going?"

"Come on." Sweet Thang's steps were brisk, yet measured. And followed.

Crossing Nostrand Avenue, at the intersection of Fulton Street, a bus almost wiped out the pair as they dodged cars like Sweet Thang dodged bullets that buzzed by his head in My Lai.

"Follow me." Sweet Thang picked up the pace.

Andy sprinted to keep up with him. "Man...you can move fast for an old drunk."

It was an old building. They bounded up two flights of stairs. Sweet Thang knocked on the door.

"Who is it?" somebody yelled.

"Sweet Thang...ass."

Andy heard the click and the door opened. Sweet Thang pushed the door. Andy followed. Andy guessed the man was in his late forties. He was a former addict, former dealer, and knew more about heroin and cocaine than anybody in Brooklyn. The room smelled of marijuana. He still had one habit.

"I need to know something." Sweet Thang's chin almost touched the man's face, and then he moved away.

Sweet Thang sat down on a coach and Andy sat next to him.

"This is the son of my closest friends...somebody stuck him with a needle and he feels that it was some kind of drug...heroine."

"What?"

"John...can you tell?"

"Come here."

Andy moved toward him, taking off his shirt. He looked at the arm. "Good, no infection...did your body ache, and muscle cramps, were you dizzy or felt nausea?"

"No."

"Good."

"Tell me man." Sweet Thang was losing his patience.

"Sweet Thang...they probably gave him heroine, but not cocaine. That is extremely habit forming. If he didn't crave another dose after 20-to-40 minutes then it wasn't coke...Do you have any cravings?"

"No."

"You must stay strong...do not surrender. I know what it takes. If you weaken a little then you'll join the walking dead on the street corner. Do I make myself clear?"

"Never."

"You may not get hooked off it with one dose, but you must always be wary. If you're strong and don't give in, then you'll be able to beat this."

"How can you tell..."

"It's my business to know...it's your business never to weaken..."

"Who did this?"

"Don't worry...I'll take care of that." Sweet Thang grabbed Andy. "Put your shirt on." They walked out as fast as they came into the room.

"Andy...Don't tell anybody, not Marvs or Golda or anybody, it'll only worry your family." They walked out of the old building and onto Fulton Street. "Remember, stay strong."

Around the corner on Bedford Avenue, Andy saw the Brownstone. There was number 1547. Mother Nature was looking out the apartment window. Sweet Thang slowed his pace and Andy's heavy breathing was forcing him to lean on the iron fence in front of the house.

"We're here." Sweet Thang opened the iron gate and Andy entered first. "Mother Nature call Golda and Marvs and tell them to get over here."

"Why?" Mother Nature leaned out the window, squinting her eyes in the early afternoon sunlight.

"Just do it!" Sweet Thang closed the gate and watched Mother Nature retreat. Andy followed Sweet Thang. He unlocked the door and walked up the steps to his apartment.

Mother Nature hung up the phone as Sweet Thang unlocked the door. "They're coming."

"Of course." Mother Nature gave him a nasty look, then turned to Andy. "Where you coming from..."

"Leave the boy alone." He directed Andy into the back bedroom and turned on the TV. Andy obeyed and closed the door. Sweet Thang plopped down on the living room couch. Mother Nature was about to say something, but changed her mind when she saw that Sweet Thang cut his eyes.

Mother Nature moved toward the room where Andy was stretched across the bed. He didn't turn on the TV, but put on the radio where Al Green's hit "Let's Stay Together" was playing. He heard the knock and said softly, "Come in."

Mother Nature opened the door, walked across the room and sat on the side of the bed. She smiled. Mother Nature stroked his head. "Andy…your mother is pretty upset."

"I know."

"Wanna talk?" Andy shrugged.

She continued stroking his head. "Andy Michael Pilgrim," Mother Nature said. He looked up.

"Everybody expects me to be perfect…no mistake Andy…but I make mistakes, and plenty. I've been shut up in that apartment, watching my neighborhood go up in flames, can't get to school, Leslie was acting stupid and when I was ready to walk out the door and go to class, I get this letter telling me that my best friend was killed in Vietnam. Then, my parents started in on me and the pressure was just too much. Mother Nature, I ran, ran, and ran some more.

"I was sitting on the stoop when Sweet Thang came by. I followed him here. Right now, I don't know whether I'm coming or going. When my parents get here, I don't know what to say or do. I don't want to go back home…"

Moments multiplied into seconds before Mother Nature gave him some much-needed support.

"Andy, relax and think about what you want to do. You got a little while to finish college, and then you can do what you want. I'm going in the next room. I won't bother you anymore. Follow your mind. This decision must be yours."

Mother Nature walked across the room and closed the door.

Andy rolled on his back and stared at the ceiling.

Chapter Forty-three

The knock.

Disoriented, Andy leaped from the bed. He staggered, tripping over a pair of shoes. The fall didn't hurt. He rubbed his eyes, realized he wasn't at home and this wasn't one of his dreams. He remembered running out of his Gates Avenue Brownstone and was in Sweet Thang and Mother Nature's place on Howard Street.

The voices he heard in the other room belonged to his parents. "Is Andy in there?" Golda pointed toward the door.

"Yeah." Mother Nature peered over her horned-rim glasses at Golda.

"I want to see him...I must talk to him and I must see what's wrong."

"Don't do or say anything stupid." Mother Nature's hand slipped off Golda's shoulders as she opened the door and walked into the room.

Andy stared.

Golda's left eyelid blinked faster than a shutter on a 35-mm camera. That nervous twitch happened when she was excited, lasted for a couple of seconds then went away.

Andy knew his mother was anxious. He continued to stare. He thought about all the times he hugged his mother when he was happy and cried on her shoulders when he was sad and especially that night when she comforted him when he didn't know if he was going to Vietnam.

It was always a battle to resist the overprotection of his parents. Sometimes, they couldn't accept he was growing up..

"Andy," Golda said as she sat on the bed.

Andy looked at his mother.

"Why did you run out the house?"

"Because."

"Andy...that's no answer."

"For me it is."

"Andy, tell me why."

"Mamma...I'm the kind of person that wants to make things happen, but you and Marvs won't let me!" Andy couldn't take his eyes off his mother. He saw the twitch. "I feel stifled. I feel controlled. Please let me be myself...let me grow up."

"Andy we want to protect you...let you grow up normally, in the middle of the ghetto. We didn't want you to be like Peter Paterson, a drop out, drug addict and derelict. We wanted the best for you..."

"I know..."

Golda reached, touched Andy's soft, closely cropped hair. She rubbed his head gently. "Andy...Andy, we love you so much. We'll do anything...it may seem like control, but it's not. We thought it was for the best. Andy, you're special. You can write. You're gifted, and we want you to use that gift."

"Mamma, I'm going to be leaving home."

"Andy!"

"Please let me finish...I'm going to Washington, DC for an interview for a job as a sportswriter with The Washington Star. I've been in contact with them for a while. I called them from school. They like my resume and the clips from the paper at City College. It's something I have to do."

His mother's eyes twitched a little longer than usual. "Andy, DC is so far..."

"Not really, I'm an hour by plane and four by train. I can come home anytime. Mamma, this is something I have to do. Will you and Marvs support me?"

Tears filled her eyes. She continued to rub his head. "My baby...leave us. It seems like yesterday that you were going out the door to Public School 305, now you're going out the door to DC.

"I was afraid then and I'm afraid now, but we'll be there for you Andy." Golda hugged Andy. She leaned back and called out, "Marvs." Marvs was at the door and heard his wife's voice. He sat down next to Andy.

"Andy...we love you."

"Our son is leaving us."

"What!"

"He's going to DC in a few days for a job interview as a sportswriter. Our boy is growing up."

"Are you sure?"

"Yes Daddy...very much so."

"If you are happy, we are happy."

"Thanks...it's going to be tough, but now that I know both of you are with me it's easier."

They hugged each other.

Chapter Forty-four

Marvs didn't want to go, but Andy encouraged his father to visit James Randall in his cell at the 57th Precinct at Gates and Lewis Avenue. When they walked up the steps to the front desk, the officer was nice and pointed the pair in the direction of the visitors' area.

In a few moments the door opened and Randall walked into the room and looked through the plate-glass panel at Marvs and Andy. He sat down and the florescent lights created a strange glow on Randall's reddish skin. He stared at Marvs while nodding his head. "Thanks for coming."

"James."

"This isn't easy for me, 'cause I respect you and your family. I'd never do anything to hurt you. What I did was for the best..."

"But to shoot Towns?"

"Yes...even that. I admitted it to the police, because I'm tired of running away from things I've done in Richmond and now here. Whatever happens from now on will just happen."

Andy leaned, and started at his father and at Randall. The conversation seemed more like a discussion of common place things like weather, rather than a shooting. The talk about murder was caught up in a matter of fact conversation. One person was hurt and it seemed Randall had some explaining to do. "Why did you shoot Towns?"

"Yes I killed the man in Richmond for cheating me out of my part of a drug deal. Towns found out because Trina's son, Peter, blabbed his big mouth...you'd better watch out for Peter, because he's deep into drugs. I wished I'd killed Towns."

"How'd he find out?"

"We were drinking in Barbara's Lounge. The conversation came up about who was the toughest. Some niggers were talking trash, well I couldn't take it anymore. I leaned over and told Peter how I killed this punk in Richmond for double-crossing me. That was a bad move.

"About two weeks later, Towns knocked on my door. He told me he had a deal for me. That if the people of the Brownstone couldn't go legally, he was going to do something that would clear everybody out so he could sell the property. He wanted me to burn the building. When I said I wouldn't, he threatened to go to the police. I decided to take matters into my own hands."

"...So when somebody wounded Towns the first time in the basement and again in his car..."

"It was Peter that shot him in the basement, because he owed him some money, but it was me that shot at his car. That Peter is a sneak. I shouldn't have trusted him...and you shouldn't either...how's Towns?"

"He's a drug dealer becoming an addict. He'll do anything for money. Trina doesn't know half the things he's done. Some of the things missing in her apartment, he stole so he could get money for his cocaine habit. He works out of a place on Lafayette Avenue.

"Be careful. I know he thinks your family has some money in your apartment. You, Golda and Andy better be careful..."

"Are you sure?"

"Positive...I don't want anything to happen to your family or any people at 423. Everybody in the building has treated me good, better than anybody in my whole life. I know I'm in for it, probable headed for death row, but that Peter is still on the loose."

The guard tapped Randall on the shoulder. "Remember what I said, be careful –watch for Peter."

"Good luck James and we'll be here for you...got a lawyer?"

"Yeah, the state will supply one...tell Golda I said hello." He got up from the chair and looked over his shoulder. "Be careful." The guard led him through the door.

Marvs and Andy got up and walked past the front desk of the precinct and into the cool night air.

"I hate leaving you and Mamma."

"Andy, you've got to go for that interview. We'll be fine."

"I don't know." Marvs and Andy walked to the car, got in, and pulled away from the curb.

They didn't see the man in the shadows.

Chapter Forty-five

Andy fast-walked through New York City's Penn Station as his legs rotated like pistons in an over-heated car. His closely cropped curly hair was parted in the middle. Andy's pecan-shaded skin was brilliant and gleaming from running. His Gates Avenue barber had given him a fresh haircut. He looked smooth in his black pinstripe suit. The off-colored red tie was impressive. He looked back over his shoulders to see Marvs close the door and drive off in the yellow cab. Andy waved to his father.

His attaché case almost tripped him; he stumbled, only to regain his balance for a few seconds, before almost tripping over a tall basketball player. The young man, about 6'5", carried a vinyl, navy blue, athletic bag that had white stripes. A pair of sneakers hung over the side. "Sorry."

The tall player nodded and both of them moved quickly in the direction of the silver Metro liner that reassembled four connecting bullets with windows. The young man bent to get his head in the car. Andy would have followed, but saw a pay phone. He had ten minutes and he wanted to make peace with Leslie. He'd called three or four times and left messages. All he got was an answering machine. He left many apologies and even a poem he'd made up.

Andy fumbled for change, dialed the number and heard her phone ringing through the receiver. Nobody answered. A recording of her voice came. Andy left another message and hung up.

Andy, standing less than six feet, sprinted through the door of the Metro liner, moved to his right and found an aisle seat. He saw the young man, a basketball player, stretch, without any effort, and take something, without any effort, from his bag in the overhead rack and then sit down in a left aisle seat about three rows up.

Andy eased into cushioned gray and black seat. He put his attaché case in his lap and in one motion pushed both spring locks so the case opened. "The New York Times, "Andy thought as he fingered through the paper to find the sports section. The newsstand had been crowded, but he'd picked up the newspaper anyway. He flipped through the pages in the sports section to find Arthur Daley's column, which was called "Sports of the Times."

Settling back, Andy pondered. "I know him... he's one of those Philadelphia Overbrook High players that came to New York last winter to play Brooklyn's Boys High in a game at Long Island University. Andy stared and resumed reading.

The Metro liner streaked to a halt at Trenton, New Jersey's capital city. People got off. People got on.

The conductor, punching tickets, walked down the aisle. The train headed into Pennsylvania and Bucks County. Andy looked at the young basketball player who reminded him of Boys High's recent Phnom, Carlton Hosch.

Andy pushed the button and his seat eased; closing his eyes and rolling his head toward the window, he drifted into a light sleep. He thought about what James Randall said about Peter. Andy hoped nothing would happen while he was spending time in DC. He prayed that the Lord protect his family. Now, his father would think about leaving Brooklyn and get the new house they saw on Long Island.

Andy realized his parents leaving Brooklyn wasn't a possibility. They loved Bedford-Stuyvesant. He was restless. His thoughts were speeding ahead of him as he thought about almost going to Vietnam, the riots, the needle that pierced his arm, and the trouble that was brewing around the Brownstone. The Metro liner shook with a clicking noise when the wheels vibrated from side-to-side as it rolled along the track in the Northern Philadelphia suburbs. Andy fell into a deeper sleep.

The conductor walked down the aisle. "Next station stops North Philadelphia...North Philadelphia is the next station."

The Metro liner pulled into North Philly Station. The conductor walked through the space between the cars and opened the door. He yelled, "Next stop is 30th Street...30th Street the last station stop in Philadelphia...30th Street," as the doors closed and the train pulled out off.

Moving through North Philadelphia, past the Philadelphia Zoo and the Museum, the Metroliner entered the station as the conductor moved into Andy's car. "30th Street, the last station stop in Philadelphia...30th Street."

Andy looked down the aisle and watched him walk. The tall basketball player jumped up, raced out the door of the Metroliner. Sprinting down the stairs, Andy watched him walk briskly into the noise of the open air corridor. The Metroliner eased out of the station, past the University of Pennsylvania, West Philly row homes near the Schuylkill River and toward Wilmington, Delaware.

Across the aisle from Andy an old Black lady stared at him. She had on a grayish hat, with a white feather sticking from the side and a veil in front. She smiled. "Where you going?"

"DC...Ma'am." Andy couldn't forget his manners.

"Uh-Huh." She was waiting for more details from Andy.

Andy smiled.

"My name is Andy Michael Pilgrim and I'm from Brooklyn. I'm graduating from City College of New York and heated for a job interview as a sportswriter in DC."

"Impressive...I like to see our young Black men...and women, achieve their dreams. You must have a wonderful mother and father."

"They're the best, but sometimes a little overprotective..."

"Honey, that's just love. We know what's out there and most of it ain't good...I'm headed from Philadelphia. My name is Mother Thomas and I'm headed for a church convention in Richmond. I have to change trains in DC...get the Southern Crescent."

"Be careful Ma'am."

"Oh, well, I'm just a talkin'. Let me let you read your paper."

Andy smiled as Mother Thomas leaned back.

Andy watched the trees, buildings and scenery create a blur as the train slowed for a split second in Wilmington before heading south toward Baltimore. Andy saw split-level brick homes on the Delaware-Pennsylvania border, not far from Chichester. For Andy, the contrast with Brooklyn was stark. Andy felt the wealthy can use their influence or money to get what they want. He was one of a few lower-middle class kids who didn't get drafted. When he went before the draft board, he was determined not to go to Vietnam, but finish college and make something of himself.

After the train left Baltimore and Metro Park, on the outskirts of Washington, he was close to his destination. Union Station in Washington D.C. The conductor opened the door. "Union Station, Washington D.C...the last stop for his train, everybody off."

Andy got up, buttoned the front of his suit, and with his left hand carried his attaché case and with the right helped Mother Thomas up from her seat and out the door.

"Young man," Mother Thomas said as Andy was walking down the platform.

"Yes 'em."

"Your mamma and daddy loves you and so do I."

Andy smiled.

Chapter Forty-six

11:30 a.m.

Andy walked through the revolving door, down a long corridor to the front desk at the Washington Star. If he was nervous, he wasn't showing it. All the years of preparation would come into play.

"Sports Department."

"Fifth floor, walk to the second elevator door, get off, walk left and take the first right door. Got all that."

"Yes," Andy lied.

He thought, I'll find it myself...a reporter must use his initiative. Well, no time is better than the present.

Andy walked through the second door, looking from side-to-side to find signs of the Star's Sports Department. The room was spacious with multi-colored desks arranged in a huge open-air newsroom. In the extreme left corner, near a series of large plate glass windows was the Sports. Andy walked briskly past the city desk area, Features and finally the Sports Department.

Near the back of the room was an old tarnished silver desk. Looking up at him was a white-haired man chain smoking cigarettes. His cigarette butts were piling up and falling over the edge of the ashtray. Andy saw him take a half butt, squash it in the pile and light another cigarette.

Andy saw a short man, wearing suspenders, walking away from the sports editor. His head was balding with a few wisps of gray hair covered the top of his head. His gray eyes gave Andy a nasty look. Andy wondered about the conversation between the two people.

Andy recognized Jack Williams, who was one of the best sports editors on the east coast. George Kerns had told him that he was called The Judge. Andy knew the editor had good feelings about him. Kerns, his friend who worked on the sports copy desk at The New York Times had told the editor about him and how he was a young Black man at a local college paper who had a flair for writing. Andy worried his lack of professional experience would hurt, but he had talent and he hoped the editor would take a chance. Andy knew if the editor liked him, he'd offer him a job today as a high school sports reporter.

Andy knew the assistant sports editor, Jonathan Barber, wasn't sure about his qualifications. Kerns told him Barber was arguing with the Judge not to hire Andy. He saw Barber walking away from Williams as he walked into the newsroom.

Barber questioned Andy's experience, but Williams was impressed with Andy's writing. He read Andy's opening paragraph of a sports story to him over the phone about a young college track runner who practiced on the runways at Kennedy airport: "On an isolated runway at one end of John F. Kennedy Airport, the tranquility is rudely disturbed by a lone figure jogging during the twilight of the early evening." That paragraph impressed the Judge.

Andy knew Barber, a southerner from Mississippi, wasn't keen on having a Black writer in the department. Kerns warned him and told Andy Barber told Williams in a conversation one day, "How're you going to hire and inexperience N...", and before he could finish his words Williams had yelled, "Stop, don't come across that way. Evaluate him on his ability, not his skin color. I don't want to hear any of that Mississippi talk in this newsroom."

Andy neared. Barber left. Williams got up, walked toward Andy.

"Good morning, Mr. New Yorker." Williams smiled, extending his hand.

"Andy Pilgrim." Andy returned a strong handshake.

"Sit down." Andy sat down, putting his attaché' case beside him. "Good trip?"

"Yes sir...left this morning on the 6:50 am Metroliner. We had a smooth ride."

"Good...Good."

"You've come highly recommended...my friend George Kerns saw some of your work and was impressed. He sent me copies and I read them. I love the feature on the kid who trained for cross-country by running on the runways at Kennedy airport...it was very insightful.

"You took an ordinary story and turned it into something special. That is a special quality and you have a good voice that the reader will really like."

"Thank you, sir."

The Judge smiled. "You don't have to call me sir, just Judge."

"OK." Andy's easy going personality sat well with the Judge, who knew he had something special. Besides, he'd have one of only three black sportswriters on the east coast. That would be a big coup for the Washington Star. Black sportswriters were hard to find.

"Andy...just a few things before we have some lunch. I want you to listen. You don't have any professional experience and that will hurt you early, but I expect you to adjust because you're a fighter.

"There are people in this department who will not like you because of your skin color. You must control your temper. If something is done against you...see me. Once they see your talent and your work ethic, they'll come over, but until then expect some hostility. It won't be easy. I have the support of the people that count and I expect you to be one of our stars."

The Judge looked hard. He saw the look of determination. Now, that hurdle was over. He smiled.

"Let's have some lunch."

"Fine with me."

The Judge got up and Andy followed. As they walked down the hallway, Managing Editor John Epps intercepted the pair. Epps was about 6-4, skinny, pale and had a lock of black hair he kept putting back into place.

"Judge."

"Yes." He turned toward his boss.

"Is this the candidate for the job?" Epps moved toward Andy and gave him a strong handshake.

"Yes sir...Andy Pilgrim." Andy smiled, extended his hand and returned a solid handshake.

"We're off to lunch...be back in a little while..."

"Good...looking forward to talking to Mr. Pilgrim. Come by my office as soon as you get back." Epps walked toward the news department area of the room.

"Will do." Judge and Andy walked toward the hallway and the elevator to the ground floor. Andy was reflective. The change in lifestyle would forever alter Andy's life: new city, new people and new relationships. How would he react to not having the people of the Brownstone in the day-to-day and moment-to-moment involvement in his life.

Andy stepped forward and opened the door to The Jailhouse Restaurant. The Judge laughed as Andy stared at the unusual décor. The restaurant booths had bars partially covering the opening; the dominant black and white colors created a kind of tongue-in-cheek atmosphere. You had to eat all of the food before you ate dessert.

"This is different."

"It is." The Judge laughed.

"Despite the look and feel, this place has the best burgers in D.C."

Andy laughed as they settled into the booth. "This is some kind of DC joke."

"Naw...just a great place to eat."

"Good."

The waitress came dressed normally, but with a prison-striped apron to carry through the prison motif. "Anything to drink?"

"A coffee and..."

"Coke for me," Andy said.

"Ready to order now?"

"Later." The Judge turned to Andy.

"We're very impressed with your work...I won't beat around the bush, we want to hire you as our high school sports writer. It's an entry-level position, but we expect you to advance and be on the college or pro beat in the future. We'll work with you and the experience you get will help you reach your goal."

Andy thought. This was what he wanted, but reality hit him—he'd be leaving Brooklyn. Telling his parents would be tough, but they'd understand and then he must tell Leslie. What would she say? More importantly, how would she react? Andy's mind raced from DC to Brooklyn and back to DC.

"Andy." The Judge looked at Andy.

"I'd be very honored to work at the Star."

The judge reached across and shook Andy's hands. The waitress came back for the order.

"Hamburger with onions and ketchup." Andy handed her the menu.

"Cheeseburger with mustard...we'll eat so we can get back and tell Mr. Epps the good news. We've got a room for you in a hotel near the paper. You can stay and watch us put the sports section together."

"That'll be great." Andy knew he made the right decision.

The Judge and Andy ate quickly and walked across the street to The Star's building, up the steps and into the newsroom and back to the office of the managing editor.

Epps was on the phone when the Judge and Andy walked through the door. He gestured for them to sit in the two chairs in front of his desk. Epps hung up the phone as they sat down. He stood up slightly, reached across the desk and shook Andy's hand. He sat back down.

"Well Mr. Pilgrim?"

"I'm here."

"Great...great, it's good to have you on board. I think we've got a good one."

"I know we have." The Judge smiled.

"Judge...when does he start?"

"He'll be at his desk on July 1, a few weeks after his graduation from City College."

"Good...Andy you have any questions?"

"The Judge told me everything. I'm impressed with everything and I've always wanted to be sportswriter and now I have the chance. I want to thank you for giving me the opportunity and especially for believing in me.

"I'd like to call my parents and tell them the good news."

"Sure by all means call your parents, it's a great moment for them, but remember Andy, it's your talent that has got you this, and in the meantime, enjoy the rest of the spring and congratulations."

Andy stood up. "Thanks." They shook hands.

Chapter Forty-seven

At his hotel room, near Pennsylvania Avenue, Andy wanted to take a nap before walking around downtown DC. It was a great afternoon. He got his sport writing job right out of college, which is incredibly hard to do, and he met a lot of the Washington Star's sportswriters. He watched how they worked and saw the kinds of stories in the paper.

Andy watched them put the paper to bed, which is a newspaper term meaning closing the paper, and realized the excitement it created would be something he'd enjoy the rest of his life.

Andy wasn't sleepy, just tired. The adrenaline rush was wearing off, but he wanted to see DC. A shower would feel good and wake him up from his little outing.

He'd go out for a while and return early enough to call his parents and Leslie. Andy got up, made it to the bathroom, and took a shower, dressed in a light blue shirt and jeans. He made sure the door was locked, sprinted to the elevator. When he got off the elevator, the lobby was crowded as he made his way out onto the street.

The rays from the sun, peeking from behind the Washington monument, were making their last appearance of the day. This city was different from New York, a different kind of rhythm. It was a place he'd have to find a way to exist. Maybe if he showed good writing skills, he'd get noticed, and be able to take his talents back to the Big Apple.

Andy squinted his eyes as he looked toward the tall, marble monument. He didn't know where he would walk, just let his instincts take over. He walked past a Jewish deli, which reminded him of Brooklyn, but it was closed. Andy peeped through the plate glass window and saw some cheesecake under a glass container. This was like the place on Nostrand Avenue before the rioters destroyed the building.

Now, he knew where to get a good pastrami sandwich mustard on rye bread. It wasn't that far from the Star.

Andy felt a tap on his shoulder. He blinked, turned to see who was behind him. A young black man flashed a gold capped smile. "Got some good stuff...make you feel good."

"No Man." Andy frowned.

"Come on try..."

"No."

Andy recalled what Sweet Thang's friend had told him. "Be Strong"

"No." Andy's glare sent the right message.

The drug dealer shrugged his shoulder and walked away.

Andy kept walking past some fast food places and then crossed several streets before he found something to eat. It was a combination bar and restaurant. Things didn't look too bad, just different.

Randy's Bar and Grill specialized in Soul Food. In the early evenings, the crowd was sparse with a few people scattered at the tables and a few more at the bar. The Juke Box was playing. Andy sat down, looked at the menu. He noticed people eating out of cooking utensils and drinking out of old mason canning jars. This was different. It must be a Washington 'Thang'. First eating in a jailhouse atmosphere and now eating out of metal pans and drinking juice out of mason jars. Andy smiled.

He moved to a table near a window to watch the people passing by. Andy wanted to get a feel for the city where he'd spend the next few years. The waitress came toward him with a gap-toothed smile. She had on a green dress, black wig, and a face shinning from sweat.

"What you having Bro?"

Andy looked at her as his eyebrows tightened. "Some baked chicken, macaroni and cheese, collard greens and sweat tea. Do you have any peach cobbler?"

"You not from around here?" Andy couldn't believe the question, but answered anyway.

'No, from Brooklyn." Andy stared

"Uh-huh…you got a job here?"

"I'll be moving here in the summer."

"Good 'cause you kind of cute with that curly hair."

Andy blushed.

"Don't get upset…just flirting a little."

"Your boyfriend might not like that."

"Who cares?"

"I do… he may come after me."

"Naw…he…working…I'll get your order and we do have peach cobbler."

"Thanks." She smiled, showing that missing tooth and walked away.

Andy dropped his head into his hands.

He got up, walked toward the jukebox. He scanned the record selections. He dropped a quarter in the slot, pushed the button for The Delfonics' "La-La Means I Love You". He walked back to his seat.

Andy looked out the window on the sidewalk, saw the young drug dealer and other people passing. He wasn't alarmed and his thoughts centered on Leslie and how he would be lonely until she transferred from Brooklyn College to Howard University. Andy listened to the lyrics. "Many guys have come to you…a line that wasn't true and you passed them by…though you're in the center ring, their line don't mean a thing, why don't you let me try…now, I don't wear a diamond ring or ever know a song to sing…All I know is La-La-La-La manes I love you…"

Andy hummed along with the Delfonics. He was happy. He thought about holding hands with Leslie walking along 125th Street at the street festival. His mother and father and how happy they were for him. He missed everybody.

The song ended: "La-La-La-La means I love you…". The waitress brought his food. She placed the small skillets on the table in front of Andy and his Coke in his mason jar filled to the top.

"Thanks." She nodded and walked away.

Andy bowed his head and said a silent blessing for the food, but most importantly a thank you for his job, his family and his girlfriend. Andy savored his food and left a generous tip.

It was dark when Andy walked out of the restaurant. He turned left, retraced his steps back toward the hotel. Andy sprinted past a sports bar and heard a loud crash. Andy glanced right and saw two guys knocking over tables and chairs. He knew from his experience in Brooklyn, bullets could fly at anytime.

Andy felt somebody behind him. Since that incident with Peter, he'd been weary. Andy glanced at a plate glass window in a store and saw a reflection of a person trailing him. Andy sped up.

The man behind him was matching his stride. Andy was alert.

"Sure you don't want my heroine?"

Andy turned. "No...don't come any closer!" The man stopped and took another step.

Andy stopped.

Andy saw the man reach for something. Andy's fist connected with the man's jaw knocking him down. He looked up at Andy from the pavement.

"Stay away I'm not a victim."

Andy backed away when he caught a glimpse of another man. "Cool it Bro...he deserved it but get outta here before some of his friends decide to investigate."

Andy turned and sprinted three blocks. He was at the hotel door in a New York minute. He pushed the revolving door, waved at the attendant at the desk and headed for the elevator.

He opened the door to his room. He walked into his bathroom, washed his face and ran cold water over his fist. That felt good.

It was time to call Marvs, Golda and Leslie.

Andy plopped down on the bed, reached for the phone, and dialed the operator to make a collect call. The phone rang on his parent's phone. Golda picked up. "Andy is that you?"

"Yes 'em, it's me. I wanted to call you and let you know everything went well. I got the job...start at over $28,000 and I'll cover high school sports..."

"Andy we're so proud of you."

"Thanks, Mamma...tell Marvs I'm leaving on the 7:30 Metroliner and be at Penn Station tomorrow around 11 a.m. Oh, by the way, has Peter been seen around the Brownstone lately?"

"Marvs will be there, and you'll know he'll be on time. As for Peter, I saw him today as I was coming from Key Foods. He looks as crazy as ever."

"He didn't say anything?"

"No he just looked and went into Trina's apartment. I kept walking. Andy...don't worry."

"Mamma I love you and Marvs."

"Love you too baby."

"See you tomorrow." Andy hung up the phone. He didn't tell his mother about the incident. That was something else he would keep a secret. Andy dialed Leslie's number.

The phone rand, rang and rang again before somebody answered the phone at the Groves household.

"Leslie?"

"No...this is her mother, Anita."

"How you doin' Mrs. Groves...its Andy."

"How you doing son?" Before Andy could answer, he heard, "Wait just a minute and I'll call her, she's out in the backyard." He just smiled.

"Baby." Leslie's voice was smooth and inviting.

"It's lonely down here in Washington. I don't know how I'm going to make it all of July and August until you get to Howard..."

"We'll make it...tell me about your new job."

"Your baby is an official sportswriter for the Washington

Star. It's all signed, sealed and delivered. I'm the high school sports writer covering all the schools in DC and the suburbs. It's a big job, but I'll handle it."

"I know you will."

"Love you, Leslie."

"Love you back, Andy."

"I think about you often...you're so special to me and I can't wait for us to be together always...What were you doing in the backyard so late?"

"Just doing something for my mother. I'm in the house now."

"Good...kind of afraid for you..."

"Don't...everything will be alright...Oh, by the way Mr. Pilgrim, you didn't look too hard at some of those pretty DC girls?"

"Oh yes I did." Andy couldn't keep from laughing.

"What." Leslie feigned with anger.

"I keep tellin' you everybody wants your curly haired man."

"Boy...you got a lot of growing up to do. Don't change the subject. Who did you meet?"

"She was kinda hall, brown skin..."

"And..."

"A Diana Ross wig on her head..."

"And..."

"And front teeth missing."

Leslie busted out laughing, startling her mother and brothers.

"Andy Michael Pilgrim...on of these days I'm going to get you back."

"She was a waitress where. I ate dinner...Leslie, you're very safe."

"Andy, don't you have to get up early?"

"Yes."

"It's almost 10:30, go to bed."

"I will...Leslie?"

"Yes Andy."

"I love you."

"Andy, and what do you know, Love you back.'"

"Can't wait to see you Leslie."

"Same here Andy...see you when you get back to Brooklyn."

"Love you."

"Love you back." Andy hung up the phone. He smiled, closed his eyes and drifted in a restful sleep.

Morning came quickly for Andy. The shrill ring from the phone startled him. It was six a.m. He showered, dressed and cleaned his hotel room. His mother always insisted they leave the room in good order. He was about to open the door when the phone rand again.

"Hello," Andy said not knowing who would be calling him this early.

"It's the Judge."

"How you doing?"

"Just wanted to say how much we're impressed with you and look forward to seeing you in July."

"I feel the same way."

"We'll send copies of the paper to you home in Brooklyn so you can keep up with the paper."

"Thanks."

"Have a safe trip." The Judge hung up the phone.

Andy placed the receiver on the base, turned off the lamp light on the light and locked the door. He got on the empty elevator and stopped at the front desk.

He checked out, grabbed a free Washington Star from the front counter. As he walked out of the revolving door, he looked but didn't see the man he'd had the confrontation with. Andy felt he must be careful. Andy felt when he returned to DC, he would be weary when he walked around the nation's capital.

Andy walked the four blocks to the train station. As he entered Union Station, he had twenty minutes before his train.

He was hungry. He saw a food stand and brought an apple Danish and coffee. He found a spot on a wooden bench and watched morning commuters scoot around the station. He couldn't wait to get home. The Brownstone on Gates Avenue would be a welcome sight, after all this change. He felt good his future was secure. All he had to do in college was pass a final exam and then endure graduation ceremony.

The time was nearing for his train. He found the entrance, walked down the staircase to the platform. He threw the coffee cup and the Danish wrapper into the garbage. He stepped onto the train, surveyed the interior of the Metroliner, saw an empty seat and walked briskly to the one next to the window. As the conductor came around to collect tickets, the train pulled out of the station. Andy realized he was leaving his DC future to return to his Brooklyn past. It was a past, which would exist a few more months.

The essence of life is change and Andy knew that his life as a young college student was over.

Now, he was moving into young adulthood. Andy drifted to sleep as the train rocked him into a dream state. Occasionally, he'd wake up to check out how close he was to New York City.

Chapter Forty-eight

Andy walked out of New York's Penn Station onto 34th Street. He looked towards Macy's Department store, then opposite to find his father's yellow cab. He saw Marvs leaning on the front hood with his favorite sweater with the alternating white, red and black triangles on the front. The back was solid black. He had on brown pants and a straw hat with a feather on the side. Andy smiled. You couldn't tell his father he wasn't cool.

Andy waved.

Marvs waved back. "Glad to have you home son." He gave Andy a hug.

Andy returned the hug. It was a bonding moment.

"Great trip...you got the job." Marvs finally said and released Andy, and in minutes they were headed to Brooklyn. Marvs glanced at Andy every few minutes and smiled.

He thought about the little seven year old kid, from a small town in Georgia, who he'd picked up at the train station. Marvs remembered those big brown eyes. He was innocent. He promised Golda he would do everything in his power to help turn that little kid into a man.

Golda and Marvs pushed Andy from where he was into a position that he could do something with his life. They saw what he could be. They saw his intelligence, potential and were determined he'd be a success.

Sometimes, Andy resented the attention, like any kid, but was smart enough to see the goal of his parents. He didn't feel like a stepson to Marvs, but his real son.

The love Golda and Marvs had for Andy was to see the possible in him, not the impossible. Love takes steps to release the power in a person's life. Now Marvs saw the power, intelligence, and God-given abilities being released in his handsome son. This wasn't his stepson, but his son. Marvs smiled.

The ride didn't take long as the cab turned the corner onto Gates Avenue. Marvs parked the car. Siting on the front stoop were Golda and Sister Love. Peter was in a chair next to the window. He heard Golda and Sister Love's conversation about Andy. Now, he was in front of him. He was angry. He saw Marvs and Andy cross the street. Andy gave his mother a hug and kissed Sister Love on the cheek.

"Boy you better give Sister Love a hug." Andy did. "Because you're a big-time sportswriter in Washington, DC, you're still my Andy. I'm gonna brag on my boy." Sister Love spoke louder. "I want the whole neighborhood to hear Andy is one of only three Black sportswriters on the entire coast. If other young black men on this block would get off their ass and do something with their lives then we'd have more boys like my Andy…Come here and give me some more suga'."

"Sister Love!"

"Don't Sister Love me… we don't brag enough on our good young men. Ain't nobody gonna bother Andy and that goes for whoever is listening." She glanced up at the window. "Golda stop worrying. Remember this old New Orleans saying 'Don't borrow trouble, wait to see what happens.'"

Golda shook her head. "Sister Love, Sister Love!"

"We're all family in this Brownstone. Andy is just as much ours as he is yours. We all helped raise him and we love him."

Andy reached out and grabbed his mother in his right and Sister Love in his left arm and led them up the stairs. His right arm felt strong. Marvs followed carrying Andy's attaché case. He glanced up and thought he saw somebody peeping.

They walked up the stairs. Sister Love stopped at the door. "Open up Jon…I forgot my key. That old fool is probably asleep. Jon! Jon!" Jon opened the door. "About time." She walked in the door, as Andy, Marvs and Golda walked up the stairs to their apartment.

Peter was in the kitchen when he heard them pass the apartment. When he felt everybody had closed the doors to their apartments, he slipped out the front door, ran down Gates Avenue, turned onto Nostrand and headed to Lafayette. Ben was waiting for him in the car.

"He's getting out of the hospital today." Peter slammed the door. "Randall's in jail and we can't do anything about him...but Towns will pay the price."

Ben sped off with the wheels of the Ford leaving rubber on the pavement and smoke in the air as the tires burned. "Stop you idiot." Peter reached back for the automatic weapon that was on the back seat and put it beside him, next to the passenger door.

Ben slowed down.

Marvs opened the door for Andy and Golda. Andy ran to his room and put his attaché case, tie and suit jacket on the bed. Golda and Marvs waited for him at the kitchen table. His mother had some sweet potato pie and milk. She leaned over and kissed him again. Andy took a bite and washed it down with cold milk. Golda knew Andy liked ice cubes in his milk. It was cold.

"We're so proud." Golda smiled, holding Marvs hand.

"I feel good I can make you and Marvs happy. The only bad thing is I'll be away from you and Marvs. I've always wanted to call you Dad..."

"No...because that makes me feel old." Marvs laughed. It was deep and came from the gut. He was a proud man and Andy made him feel even prouder.

"OK...Marvs," Andy said.

"The only thing we're concerned about is getting you a place in DC," Marvs said.

"I think we have a solution to the problem," Golda added. "I have some people in DC and we'll get you a place. We'll carry your things in June and get you in your own place before the first of July."

"Oh, I meant to ask you, how's Leslie taking this?"

"It was hard for her, but she realized it's for the best...in fact, she may come to DC in the fall for her last year at

Howard University. That would be good."

"I hope things work out, but..."

"I know what you two are thinking." Andy took another bite of pie. "We're just a few hours from each other...if it's meant to be we'll find a way. Wasn't that the saying you always told me. Love is like holding a dove. If you hold it too tight, you'll squeeze it to death. If you don't hold it, it'll fly away. You have to hold it just right."

"You actually listened to some of things I said." Golda smiled at Andy.

"Mamma listen."

"Things will work out for you two...in fact I have a surprise for you and Leslie."

"Really."

"I was picking up fares in midtown when this man got in my cab. We talked and I told him about you. He listened and then he said for somebody who is trying to make it, he wanted to do something. I couldn't figure out what he was talking about.

"He said he was the director of the Broadway show 'Hello Dolly...'"

"Wow... that's the show everybody wants to see at City College. It has the new all black cast of Pearl Bailey and Cab Calloway. That's where the hit song 'Before The Parade Passes By' is from, but nobody can get tickets."

"Well, Mr. Andy Michael Pilgrim." Marvs reached in his pocket and handed Andy two Orchestra seats for tomorrow evening's performance. Andy thought this would be the perfect time to give Leslie his present he'd been keeping for almost a year.

Marvs reached across the table and gave Andy two tickets. The look on his face was what he wanted to see. Golda squeezed Marvs' hand and gave him a kiss.

The late afternoon sun caused Ben's eyes to squint as the car moved along Jamaica Avenue. Peter look straight ahead. Ben turned onto Philips Street and stopped the car. He looked down the street. Peter reached over and grabbed the automatic weapon. He laid it across his lap.

"There!" Peter pointed.

"I see." Ben said.

Ben turned on the ignition and the car moved slowly down the tree-lined block. Towns was standing in the doorway looking up and down the street.

"He's scooping," Ben said.

"I know," Peter answered. "Park the car."

Ben pulled over, close to the curb, about five houses from where Towns was standing. Peter and Ben looked intently.

The gun weighted heavy on Peter's legs. Nothing would deter him. Finally, he'd get rid of Towns.

The stalk was on.

Peter saw Towns take a step out of the doorway, down the steps and onto the street. There was nobody in sight, except for Towns. He nudged Ben and he started the car. Ben maneuvered the car out of the parking spot and in three seconds he was at top speed. Peter raised the gun off his legs into shooting position. He squeezed the trigger. The bullets riddled Towns body. He was sprayed by rapid-fire gunfire. He lay sprawled on the curb in front of his house. Ben turned the corner as Peter placed the automatic weapon on the floor of the Ford. They drove on Jamaica Avenue toward Brooklyn.

"We're not finished...there's one more." Peter smiled. "I've got plans for Andy Michael Pilgrim."

Chapter Forty-nine

On a clear Wednesday evening, a cool breeze swept down 43rd Street in midtown Manhattan. It was twilight and the sun was disappearing behind the New York City skyscrapers. Andy, in his light blue Nehru shirt and navy blue pants, and Leslie, in a watercolor blue dress, emerged from the subway.

Andy squeezed Leslie's hand as they headed down 43rd toward Broadway. The reservations were for six for the show and an 8:30 curtain time. The décor was typical Chinese with paintings, fans, and very dark lighting. The deep red cushioned seats had black trim. The waitress escorted the pair to their booth. Andy thought, "At least she had all her teeth, unlike the waitress in DC."

The booth was comfortable. "Anything to drink?"

"Thank you." She handed each a menu.

"I know what I want." Andy closed the menu, as Leslie continued to scan her list of dinner items. "You seem a little down, baby."

Leslie took a last glance and closed her menu. She looked at Andy. She was deep in thought. "I hope we can make this work Andy. You're starting a career in a new city. There's the distance..."

"Leslie, it'll be only for a month and with you applying for Howard, you'll be there in the fall. I'm going to see you every weekend. If we want to make this work, we will find a way."

"I feel like I'm losing my love..."

"No you're not. Don't even think that."

"I know, but so many things are happening..."

"...and we have to change with 'em."

"Andy...do you love me?"

"Yes I do...and I always will." Andy reached, clasped her hands. He pulled them to him and kissed her fingers.

"Andy...Andy."

"I will love you with all my heart...what I always say?...I love you back."

The waitress stepped toward the table. "Are you ready to order?"

"We'll have Sweet and Sour Shrimp, Chicken Chow Mien and some Wonton Soup, please."

"Thank you." She walked away giving the food order in Chinese to the waiter.

"Leslie, I have something for you." Andy reached in his pocket and pulled out a small present, the one he rehearsed giving her when he was in Central Park.

"Open it."

Leslie smiled and unwrapped the gift. "What is it?"

"Be patient and open it."

Leslie pulled out two gold chains. What was unusual was that they were attached to one piece of jewelry. It was a heart with a key inside. There was a thin piece of gold connecting the two pieces.

Andy reached for her hand with the gold heart in her fingers.

"We'll break it together and each will keep a piece and put it around the others neck. I'll put the heart around my neck and you put the key around your neck..."

"Andy, what does it say on the front?" Leslie fingered the heart.

"It says 'Whoever holds the key, holds the key to my heart.'"

A tear came to Leslie's eyes. Andy reached up and wiped them. They twisted the two gold pieces until they separated.

Leslie put the gold chain with the heart around Andy's neck.

Andy put the gold chain with the key around Leslie's neck.

Each leaned. They kissed. As they sat down, each smiled.

"Andy, it's incredible...I'm speechless. It says so much about our relationship."

The waitress interrupted them with their food order. As

they ate, the moment was long, sensual and intoxicating. The next time they saw the waitress she had their check. Andy paid the bill and escorted Leslie onto Broadway. The Saint James Theatre was a block away. It was about thirty minutes before curtain time and the theatre district, around Schubert's Alley, was bustling as people headed toward "Purlie", "Pippin" and other musicals.

On West 44th, people headed toward the marquee with Pearl Bailey as Hello Dolly and Cab Calloway as Horace Vandergelder in bright lights. They walked into the theatre. Andy handed the tickets to a man in a dark black suit. They walked to their orchestra seats. The matron at the door handed Andy two playbills, the official program of the theatre.

Andy and Leslie moved toward their seats. It was light enough for them to read their playbills which talked about the two stars that captivated Broadway in this all-black version of Hello Dolly which Carol Channing had made famous. The producers had decided to tap into the black audience. Pearl Bailey was an amazing actress/singer. She starred in such movies as "Porgy and Bess", "Carmen Jones" and "St. Louis Blues". Her co-star, Cab Calloway, was a legendary song and dance man. He'd become the king of "Hi-De-Hi-De-Ho" and stared in "Stormy Weather" and "Porgy and Bess."

When the curtain went up, Andy and Leslie saw and American Musical that brought a whole different atmosphere to Broadway. It was electric. Bailey and Calloway stopped the show many times, and when they did the famous "Hello Dolly" number, the audience demanded three encores.

As the curtain went down, Andy and Leslie were exhilarated along with the rest of the audience. There were more curtain calls. Pearl Bailey and Cab Calloway came back on stage and performed several songs they'd made famous in the fifties and sixties. Few people could be called legends, but on the Saint James stage that Wednesday night two of the greatest black performers transformed the evening into a magical event.

When Leslie and Andy walked out onto 44th street, he pulled her left toward Broadway instead of the right toward the Eight Avenue subway.

"Where we going?"

"To a wonderland, my princess, to a fantastic wonderland…"

"A what?"

"Just follow me." Andy and Leslie walked arm-in-arm up Eighth Avenue toward Central Park. The leisurely stroll carried them past the movie theatre that was showing Steve McQueen in "The Sand Pebbles" and some shows they wanted to see. There was even a place called "Orange Julius" where Andy bought Leslie an orange drink.

He bought a single drink and both alternated sipping from the same straw.

It was about eleven when they reached Columbus Circle, 59th and Eighth, and the horse and carriages were lined up waiting for customers.

"Andy."

"That's right, we're going for a ride around midtown to see the sights of Central Park." Andy paid the driver and he helped Leslie get in the carriage. The ride was slow. The two lovers held hands and kissed. Leslie fingered the heart around Andy's neck and the key around her neck.

The night was clear and you could see the stars, despite the bright lights from the tall skyscrapers. The romantic carriage ride carried the lovers through the edge of Central Park, down Eighth Avenue, almost to the midtown theatre district and back up Broadway. The clop-clop of the horse's metal shoes hitting the pavement was very soothing. The swaying ride was the right touch to end the evening.

"I don't mean to be a spoil sport, but are we going to take the subway this late to Brooklyn?"

"Nope…our cab should be right up there at the corner of 59th and Broadway." There was Marvs leaning against the cab.

Andy helped Leslie down from the carriage and gave the driver a tip.

"Marvs...right on time."

"12:15 a.m."

Leslie shook her head. "You two...like father, like son."

Marvs opened the back door for them. He got in on the driver's side. "I can see everything in my rear-view mirror...none of that hanky-panky." Everybody smiled.

"How'd you like the necklace?"

"It's fantastic, Mr. Pilgrim."

"Good...he saved a long time for that. I thought it was different. I haven't seen anything like that."

The cab ride was quick as Marvs pulled into Leslie's block.

Andy got out first and opened the door for his girlfriend. He walked her to the door and gave her a quick goodnight kiss.

"Thanks for the beautiful evening...Andy."

"Yes."

"I love you."

"I love you back."

"We'll make it...I know we will."

Andy watched her close the door and then he walked back to the cab. He got in the front seat with this father. "I just knew you weren't going to get in the backseat...I'm your personal driver."

"Thanks Marvs...for everything."

"You're welcome, son."

Marvs parked the car, as he always did, across the street from the Brownstone. He could always look out during the night to see if anything or anybody was messing with the car.

While crossing the street, they didn't see the pair of eyes watching them. Going up the stairs Marvs headed for the apartment while Andy kept going until he reached the door that lead to the roof.

"Where's Andy?"

"Gone up on the roof like he's always done since he came

from Georgia. I think it reminds him of down south."

"I wish he wouldn't go up there."

"He'll be alright, anyway let me tell you about Mr. Andy." Golda smiled, but deep inside she was worried.

Andy left the door to the narrow staircase open. The cool breeze wiped the sweat off his face. He walked to the edge of the roof and looked toward Franklin Avenue where they had some of the best delicatessens in the borough. There was Marcy Park where he could play a game of hoops, and to the east, Manhattan with the skyline. Around him was his own neighborhood of Bedford-Stuyvesant, not Manhattan Beach, Brooklyn Heights, Bay Ridge, Midwood, Williamsburg, Park Slop or even Flatbush where the Dodgers played baseball. Besides, The Mets were the best. That's a laugh, the Mets had had a winning season in their history.

He thought about Peter and how they used to be friends. Jealousy can destroy. Jealousy can kill a friendship. When Andy had first arrived from Georgia, Peter was the person who showed him friendship. He showed him who could be trusted in the streets and who to stay away from in the neighborhood. Bedford-Stuyvesant was cruel to young black men. Easy money was there for the making, but it could mean death if you crossed the wrong drug dealer.

Sometimes, Peter would come up on the roof with Andy. Peter would talk about the money that could be made. Andy would say, "But those are the very same people you wanted me to stay away from and yet you're out there with them."

Gradually, Peter and Andy separated. Both dreamed, with one being patient while working for his dream and the other wantingit now. They'd drifted in two directions.

Andy walked around the roof. He thought about Leslie, Marvs, Golda, DC and the future away from the Brownstone in Brooklyn.

He walked around the roof humming the tune from The Drifters latest song, "Up On The Roof." Andy stared to sing, "When this old world starts getting me down and people are just too much for me to face…I climb way up to the top of the stairs and all my cares just drift into space…On the roof…the only place I know…where you just have to wish to make it so…I get away from the hustling crowd and all that rat-race noise in the streets…Up on The Roof."

Andy was into the song and didn't recognize the noise, but then the whistling sound startled him. He threw his body, hard, on the roof and started to crawl until he got to the entrance. He slid over the edge, righted himself and scampered down the steps.

Andy banged on the door. Golda opened it quickly.

"Andy, what happened?"

"I think somebody shot at me."

"They did what!"

"Shot at me!"

Marvs ran and closed the curtains on the front and Golda did the same on the back, also checking to see if the window was locked going to the fire escape. The family sat down at the kitchen table and talked. The phone rang. Everybody held their breath for a second. Golda answered. It was Mother Nature.

"Just wanted to see if Andy got back, hadn't heard from you in a couple of day."

"Yes…Andy doing good and got that job."

"Great."

"Something's just happened."

"You sound nervous, Golda…tell me."

"Somebody shot at Andy!"

"Where…how!"

"He came home from his date with Leslie and went on the roof, like he always does. Then he came running to the door…"

"Everybody alright?"

"Yes…we're in for the night. We're going to decide what to do." Golda hung up the phone, reached across the kitchen table to Andy's hand.

Mother Nature hung up the phone, walked to the living room and told Sweet Thang. He didn't say a word, but knew he had to protect Andy.

Both sat and stared at each other. The radio was on when they heard the news reporter say, "And now in local news, brought to you by your KEY foods supermarket... There's been a drive-by shooting in Jamaica, Queens. Phillips Street is a quiet residential street in Queens and today that street was shocked when entrepreneur Jesse Towns, who was recovering from gunshot wounds from a previous shooting, was gunned down in front of his home. This was the third attempt on his life, and this time the killer was successful. Towns has been in the news before when his wife was found killed and stuffed in a trunk a few years ago. Police are investigating..."

Mother Nature reached, turned the knob. Silence.

Chapter Fifty

The early weekday morning sunlight washed Andy's face. He squinted his eyes to keep out the bright light. He waited for Golda's voice from the kitchen. Andy counted the seconds, because his sixth sense told him she'd be calling his name in a few moments.

"Andy...Andy honey, it's time to get up."

Andy smiled.

He jumped out of bed and said to himself, "Right on time," then headed toward the bathroom. He closed the door behind him and yelled, "I'm up Mamma."

"Good, it's Wednesday and we need some fresh fish. Make sure you get small Whiting. You know Marvs loves the small ones. Get about twelve, because somebody will be dropping in on fish day...they always do. Hopefully, Joshua will have some to day."

Andy's friend, Joshua, a white merchant who rebuilt the fish market after the black rioters had destroyed the inside of his establishment, was working again.

Andy dreaded seeing Joshua.

He was a man in his mid-fifties who had sold Andy's family fresh fish since he arrived from Georgia. He was one of the white businessmen hurt most by the rioters. Seeing Joshua wouldn't be easy.

Andy came out of the bathroom and dressed quickly. He came to the kitchen table as Golda was turning away, putting some milk into the refrigerator

"The funds Mamma." Golda looked at Andy. "Mamma, the money."

"Oh...here's ten, which should cover everything." Andy grabbed the money out of his mother's hands as he planted a kiss on her cheek.

"Get back quick...wait, I'll walk you down the stairs,

'cause I've got to see Trina for a few minutes." Andy closed the door behind his mother.

He didn't speak. "Morning Peter," Golda said to get his attention.

"Oh, good morning Mrs. Pilgrim."

"At least he got some manners...get your butt back here, and don't stop at that no-good friend of yours house." Peter slammed the door and headed in the same direction that Andy had walked a few minutes earlier.

Golda walked into Trina's apartment. There were children clothes all over the floor, tables and chairs. "Have to iron today." Trina walked ahead of Golda picking up clothes.

"Somebody shot at Andy last night."

Trina looked at Golda. "What!"

"You heard me... somebody shot at Andy when he was up on the roof. He's all upset, but won't show it."

"Golda, not Andy."

"Yes, Andy...Trina we have to talk." Trina looked hard at Golda without blinking an eye.

Andy turned the corner onto Nostrand Avenue and headed toward the fish market. Each step brought him face to face with a person he dreaded holding even the slightest conversation with. This was going to be tough.

The neighborhood people were back shopping on Nostrand Avenue.

For the first times in weeks, since the riots, people felt comfortable enough to come out and shop in one of the business areas of Bedford Stuyvesant. The White merchants were back, a little resentful and less friendly, but back in their rebuilt stores. People were buying the essentials, such as the food stables, flour, sugar and salt. Even the Chinese laundry was open.

Andy walked briskly down Nostrand enjoying the warm sunny day in May. There wasn't a cloud in the sky, yet Andy sensed a shadow lurking. He couldn't figure out what it was. He couldn't tell if it was a person or thing hovering over him.

Everything was going so good. His relationship with Leslie, graduating from City College in June and a firm job offer in DC. He had made his parents proud. These should've been exhilarating days in Brooklyn which he would remember and wanted to remember for the rest of his life.

Yet, there was something. His thoughts were negative, something he's never allowed to enter his thinking. Andy felt sad because things in his life, the Brownstone people and even the familiar places would be different. This wasn't the feeling he wanted at this moment, it was a sensation that haunted his thoughts. It was like the children's nursery rhythm where everything was perfect until the shadow of the spider came into view.

Andy knew there was a negative shadow somewhere, closer than he would like to think, that seemed ready to blot out this bright sunshine in his life.

The fish market was two stores on the right. As he walked, he tried to envision the conversation that his mother and Trina were having back in the Brownstone. Golda's facial features showed a quiet calm, but inside she was agitated at Trina's conversation.

Trina was straining to remain calm. She was uncomfortable, as if she was hiding something.

"Trina."

"Yeah."

"What's going on with Peter, he's been doing some crazy things lately with Towns and that bunch. I feel he's not finished. I fear for Andy, especially after somebody shot at him last night."

Trina looked, but didn't answer.

Golda stared. He eyes never blinked.

The silence was stifling. Golda wasn't leaving Trina's apartment until she had some answers. There weren't going to be any more sleepless nights.

First, there was Towns trying to sell the Brownstone out from under the residents, then the riots destroying any sense of community in Bedford Stuyvesant, and then Randall killing Towns and finally somebody shooting at Andy.

Golda leaned forward in her chair. "Talk to me Trina, I want some answers."

Trina knew the information she was about to reveal to Golda would be troubling to everybody in the Brownstone. She knew the truth must come out, and it might as well be now.

"Golda..." Trina leaned forward bringing her face within inches of Golda. Trina whispered in her ear. Golda fell back in her chair.

At the same time, Andy opened the door to the fish market and received a surprise smile from Joshua.

"Andy, my boy." The silver-haired, slightly overweight man with the white apron looked up from behind the glass counter.

"Joshua." Andy walked into the store, the odor of fresh fish permeating every corner, and extended his hand over the counter. The handshake was firm.

"It's good to see you. When I saw your smile, I knew your mother, Golda, with the Jewish name, wants her Whiting and she wants them small."

"Yeah, ten to twelve depending on the size. My father loves them small." Joshua 's green eyes followed Andy as he moved along the counter, looking at the large variety of fish from sea bass, croaker, flounder, cod and everything that could be caught at sea. Joshua had large shrimp and some squid for the few Asian families in the area.

"It'll take me a few minutes to get the Whiting fish ready. I don't get much business these days...not since the rioters looted my store." Joshua reached into the chilled fish case, the one with the ice almost covering the fish, and started taking out the best Whiting.

Andy studied the man's face, which had a few more wrinkles, and more space between his forehead and his hairline. "Joshua...I'm glad you decided to keep your business in Bedford-Stuyvesant and not move it to Queens or Long Island. A lot of people didn't stay after the riots and our community is suffering. Key Foods, Brandy's Jewish bakery, and even Auckerman's candy store have put up a closing sign. You have to catch a bus to find anything you need."

Joshua placed the last fish onto the waxed paper, wrapped it neatly in brown paper, and sealed it with tape. "I'm going to give it a try...a lot of people don't want white owned businesses on Nostrand Avenue anymore. My wife and my family want me to move my business. They say 'stay and die' but I told them I'm not running from anybody or anything. I put too much into this place to let a few thugs chase me away from my customers."

Andy considered Joshua's facial expressions. There was anger, frustration and finally resignation. "We do...we want you to stay. You're a part of our lives. When I came from Georgia, you taught me with your kindness that all white people aren't racist...that you must not judge everybody on their skin color, but by who they are. You don't realize it, but that was an important lesson. From you Joshua, I learned trust.

"I hope to return the favor to you...all Black people aren't thugs, looters and killers. And all Black people don't want you to leave..."

"Andy, you're quite a young man, but the entire world doesn't think like you."

"When I saw the flames on Nostrand Avenue, and all the looting, I knew it was wrong. The people who were getting hurt were just like us. My family prayed that your shop wasn't damaged, and if it was, that you could build it back."

Joshua's intense look was not hostile, just trying to figure out this young Black man standing in front of him. "It's because of you, your family and others that I did come back...besides where would Golda get her fish?

"Enough already about the troubles of the world. For you my boy, what is your future?"

Andy was relieved the conversation changed.

"I'll be a college graduate in a month and then I'm headed for DC in July to work as a sportswriter with the Washington Star."

"A big time writer, yes...you won't forget your old-friend, Joshua?"

"Never, you're one of the special people in my life."

Joshua put the fish on top of the counter as Andy handed him eight one-dollar bills. Joshua gave him less than a dollar in change for the Whiting.

"Thank you." Andy walked toward the door. He turned to face Joshua and started to say something when Joshua said, "Andy, when I saw the looting, the flames eating at the buildings and the people yelling, 'Burn-Baby-Burn', I hated all Black people. Andy, I still feel I was wronged for no reason, but you and your family reminded me that there still is hope.

"My family fled Poland after World War I to get away from the oppression and the police coming in the night and beating up Jews and burning their homes and places of business. When I saw the riots on TV, it brought back memories. But when I see you, Golda, Marvs and others, it brings the good back inside me.

"Now as for you, the grown-up man, good luck and keep in touch."

Andy walked back to the counter. "I'll send you copies of the articles I write, but I don't know where to send them...what if I mail them to the store?"

"Wait." Joshua reached in the cash register and then handed Andy a business card with his home address. "Just in case I close the fish market. Andy, you and your family are still my friends."

Joshua walked from behind the counter and gave Andy a big hug.

Andy smiled as he put the business card in his pocket, then walked out the door. Joshua waved—he knew his future in Bedford-Stuyvesant wasn't long.

Andy had one more stop to make before he headed back home. Instead of going straight back to the Brownstone, he walked in the direction toward the Jamaican Sweet Shop. He wanted to surprise Golda with some fresh coconut bread. This would be a special treat. Andy walked at a quick pace. He thought he heard footsteps, but it was probably just his imagination. He glanced over his shoulder and thought he caught a glimpse of Peter Paterson, but the person quickly ducked into an alleyway between two buildings.

What Andy didn't see moving in his direction slowly down the street was a police car. Then, he saw the flickering lights from on top of the black and white car. He heard sirens. He thought it was just another day in the ever-dangerous streets. He froze when he heard "freeze" as two policemen jumped out of the closet car and headed in his direction. Andy dropped the fish onto the pavement as they pushed him against a wall. He was numb. This must have been happening to someone else.

Andy leaned over, palms pushing hard on the brick wall. From the corners of his eyes he could see people staring. He was in the spread eagle position with his legs extended far apart. This position hurt. What hurt more was his pride as the policeman felt his chest and then lower between his legs and down to his calves. He'd seen policemen do this to other people, but here and now it was happening to Andy Michael Pilgrim.

They searched him.

A third officer, yelling, came from a police car trailing the lead car: "That's not him." The officer stopped his search, mumbled an apology and sprinted back to the police car.

"Be on your way," he yelled over his shoulder.

Andy pulled his legs together, turned away from the wall to face the other officers. As fast as it had happened, the search ended. People stared. Andy reached down, picked up his package, gathered courage, and asked, "Officer...what did I do?"

"Nothing. We had to make sure." They went back to their cars, jumped in, slammed doors and left the scene on screeching tires as the rubber met the Nostrand Avenue pavement.

Andy looked at his hand clutching the package and saw it was trembling. He kept walking toward the sweet shop.

At that moment Golda felt a chill that made her push back against the recliner.

Trina admitted that Peter abhorred Andy. In his eyes Andy was a mamma's boy who got all the breaks. Peter was jealous. He hated Andy for his success in college, having a girlfriend and what he was doing with his life. He wanted Andy to leave Brooklyn in a casket, not on a train. He had been plotting to kill him for a long time, and after he had helped Randall kill Towns, Peter found the courage to plot Andy's death. He shot at Andy last night to scare him, but the next time he wouldn't miss.

Trina continued. "Peter not only helped kill Towns, but helped plot his murder."

"What?"

"Yes..."Tears rolled down Trina's face. "My son is a murderer." Golda hugged Trina.

Golda didn't know how long they were in this position.

The knock at the door surprised both women.

"Who is it?" Trina yelled.

"It's me, Andy."

"Oh my baby." Golda moved quickly to the door. "I'm going now, Trina...keep strong. I'll be back in a few minutes."

Trina kept talking as Golda moved quickly to the door. "I'm sorry...I'm sorry, I should've told somebody. If something happens to Andy..." Trina fell back onto to chair and sobbed.

"You can't help what your children do...only guide them." Golda opened the door. "I'll comeback in a few minutes and we'll figure out something." She reached out and hugged Andy.

"What's wrong with Miss Trina?" They walked up the steps. "Here's the fish and I bought you some coconut bread...Mamma the cops frisked me when I was walking down Nostrand."

"What!"

"They thought I was the Black person who did something at the fish market...Mamma, somebody shot Joshua!"

Chapter Fifty-one

Golda opened the door to the apartment, pushed Andy inside. "Sit down." She walked through the living room into the kitchen and put the Whitings and coconut bread on the counter. She came back into the living room, sat down next to Andy on the couch, reached out and touched his hands.

"Turn the radio off, 'cause I want to talk." Andy was about to turn the knob when the WBLS-AM disc jockey shrieked, "We have a news flash!" Andy pulled his right hand back. "As if the riots in Bedford Stuyvesant hadn't destroyed a community's morale, the already fragile peace has been shattered by a shooting on Nostrand Avenue near the corner of Gates Avenue."

Andy squeezed his mother's hand tighter, looked at her, closed his eyes and leaned back on the couch. His hand never left his mother's grip.

The DJ continued, "Long-time fish market owner, Joshua Bernstein's shoulder was wounded early this morning. Bernstein tried to fight off a thief to prevent the robbery of his newly refurbished store. His store, which had been heavily damaged in the riots, was open only two weeks when this incident happened today. Bernstein was one of a handful of white businessmen who returned to Nostrand Avenue after the riots.

Golda squeezed Andy's hand tighter as the encounter continued, "Mr. Bernstein was in stable condition at Kings County Hospital. He vowed to reporters at the scene that he was not leaving Bedford Stuyvesant. In his own words he said, 'There are too many good people to leave…nobody with a gun is going to run me away.' That was from a very brave man…and in other news in the BIG Apple…"

Andy smiled as he turned the knob on the radio to the off position

Golda reached out and hugged Andy. "Baby...you're in danger!" Andy looked deep into his mother's eyes. Golda wanted to keep her eyes on Andy every minute, but she knew that was impossible.

While Golda and Andy talked in their apartment, two floors down Trina cried alone. Trina, still sitting in the recliner, jumped when she heard the door slam. "Who is it?" she said, shaking.

"Me."

"Me who?"

"Peter." Trina was at the kitchen door. "Where you been boy?...What you been doin'?"

"Out."

"Huh...repeat that."

"Out."

"Out where...don't bring me no attitude."

"I ain't got no attitude...now...just get out of my face and stop questioning everything I do." Trina moved closer. Peter's dark skin, which usually had a reddish tint was now flushed. His large eyebrows were arched and nostrils flared. Peter's bluish-black lips were bleeding at the corner. He was 6-2 and when you glanced at him, the age of twenty wouldn't cross your mind.

"Why you bleedin' boy?"

"I told you, don't question me." Peter started to move when Trina snatched his shoulder, bringing the rest of his body with him. "What you doin'?" ...you respect me nigger!" Trina wasn't crying anymore; now she was mad and almost hysterical.

"Boy, you crazy...I know...you can't do anything to me, 'cause your mother and I grew up on the streets...you goin' to talk to me today, no more games from you...you gonna talk to me now...what the hell you mean shootin' at Andy last night?"

Peter tried unsuccessfully to get away from his mother who outweighed him by almost thirty pounds. She had both hands with a tight grip on his shoulders. Peter struggled. "Answer me boy…I know all about you and Randall plotting Towns' murder down in his apartment." Something came into Trina's head. It was something that hadn't crossed her mind for a long time. "It was you…you shot Towns the first time down in the basement. I thought I recognized your bony ass running out the front door.

"What have I birthed into the world?"

Peter remained defiant. "You brought a man into the world that takes care of his own business…"

Trina shouted at the top of her voice, "You stupid idiot. I birthed a jealous murderer. You dropped out of school, got on drugs, couldn't keep a job…and you are a killer."

Peter finally snatched himself away from his mother. "Yes…and I'm glad. All I've ever heard from you is Andy this and Andy that. This whole building put me down. Well, there won't be any Andy anymore…" He turned, sprinted toward the door and down the stairs.

Trina screamed, "Peter!" She heard the front door slam.

Peter ran out the front door, stopped, and said something to some men. Trina could only hear the voices, but then she recognized the uniforms of the policemen. She stepped back and closed the door.

A few seconds later, Trina heard footsteps pass her door and continue up the stairway.

Golda responded to the hard knocking on her door. "Yes."

"Open up…it's the police."

Golda swallowed.

"Open up or we'll knock the door down."

Golda got up from the couch, and moved toward the door. "Here I come." She peeped through the keyhole and saw angry white faces.

"Open up!"

"What you want, we haven't did anything wrong."

"Open up now."

Andy moved toward his mother. "Mamma, open the door

and let them in, please don't make matters worse. We'll get out of this."

Carefully, Golda pushed back the slide latch, and then unlocked the door. The policemen pushed hard, almost knocking Golda down. They moved straight for Andy with guns pointing. "Hands up!"

Golda watched in horror. She felt a wetness dribble down her legs. She couldn't stop the flow of urine. She wanted to scream, but couldn't. She started to cry, "My baby...my baby!"

Andy put his hands up above his head. He was in shock.

One policeman put handcuffs on him. His wrist hurt. As he moved his hands, the handcuffs cut deeper into his circulation.

Golda finally got a sound to come out her throat. "Why you taking my boy?"

"Somebody robbed the fish market and shot the owner," a policeman said. "We have an eyewitness who said that this boy did it."

"Who?"

"We can't tell you ma'am, but he'll be at the 57th Precinct."

The police left with Andy in front as they walked down the stairs. Golda rushed to the stairs. She gripped the banister as she shrieked. The screaming brought Sister Love and Trina out their apartments. Golda rushed back to the window and saw Andy being pushed into the police car. She caught a glimpse of Peter across the street, smiling.

Sister Love and Trina came into the apartment. They got Golda back to the couch.

"What happen?" Sister Loved asked.

"They arrested Andy for shooting Joshua, the fish store owner. They said he tried to rob the store...my baby's in jail."

"That's a lie." Sister Love was angry.

"Calm yourself, we'll get this straight." Trina looked toward the window. "Sister Love, call Marvs job and get in touch with him. I've got to do something."

Sister Love called Marvs while comforting Golda who was totally hysterical now.

Trina walked toward the door. "I'll be back." She ran down the stairs and out the front door. Across the street Peter had his back to the Brownstone. He was about to walk down the street when Trina grabbed him. "Bring your ass back here." Peter tried to pull away. "Move and I'll kill you on the spot nigger." Trina squeezed Peter's arms as she pushed him back across the street to her apartment.

When they got to the apartment, Trina pushed Peter through the door. "You did your last evil deed. You're my son, but you're evil and you're not going to destroy Andy or anybody else. I know you told the cops and I'm going to call somebody who will make you tell the truth. Sit in that chair. If you try to run, I'll kill you. I birthed you. And I can kill you." Peter knew his mother meant every word. He watched as his mother dialed the number. "Sweet Thang, this is Trina, get your ass over here now…don't ask any questions, just get over here." She stepped toward Peter and sat down in her recliner in front of him.

Outside the apartment she heard screeching wheels. It was Marvs. She heard him run up the steps to the apartment. Golda's scream let him know that she was in the apartment. She rolled her eyes at Peter. "Nothing better happen to Andy…I don't know why you're jealous, but I'm going to find out. Your days for causing trouble are over."

Andy was alone.

He sat in the back of the police car staring straight ahead. All he could see was his mother crying and how helpless she looked. He was surrounded by steel on both sides and bulletproof glass in front of him. His wrists ached. The physical pain was horrible, but for the first time in his life he was isolated from loving human contact.

There was light around him, but he might as well be in a coffin. He was controlled by outside forces telling him when to breath, eat, move, and talk. The numbness engulfed his whole being.

The police car motored down Gates Avenue toward Atwater Street. He saw the precinct on the left. It was the same place that he and his father had to come to see Randall. What a difference from being in a cab to being in a police car.

When the car pulled into the back of the precinct, Andy's body tensed. His mind almost shutdown. He was going on instinct. When the car stopped, and the policeman opened the door, he felt his life was over.

The policeman led him to a desk, where a cop booked him. He then moved him closer to a wall. The policeman unlocked the handcuffs and instructed him to put his hands on the wall. Andy felt like Déjà vu, like earlier in the day when he'd done the same thing. He was spread eagle, arms and legs spread. The policemen took off his belt, emptied his pockets and put everything in a plastic bag.

Andy didn't say a word as the policeman moved his hands over his chest, between his legs and used a Billy club to direct his every action. He had to take off his shoes and socks.

Andy felt degraded.

The policeman led Andy to a temporary holding cell. He was alone without any human contact. He was isolated from his family, friends and the rest of the world. Andy sat on a bench, put his back against the wall, pulled his knees to his chest and closed his eyes.

Andy cried.

He wasn't the only one crying. Golda was hysterical. Sister Love helped her get into the bathroom. Golda changed her underclothes and washed up. She had stopped screaming and was making a low moan.

Marvs turned the key and opened the door. "Golda." She almost knocked Sister Love against the wall in trying to get to Marvs. She threw herself into his arms. "Our boy is in jail...Oh my God." He held her tight and calmed his wife before trying to get any information. Sister Love came into the living room as Marvs led Golda to the couch. She sat down with her head on his chest.

Downstairs, Trina just looked at Peter. "You're disgusting...Jealousy ain't good enough, there's got to be another reason.

"It's your fault for not going to school. All your lazy ass wanted to do was cut classes, drink 40-ounce beers and smoke dope. We tried to help you, but you wouldn't do anything...always looking for the short cut. This is what the short cuts got you, a murder one rap and the rest of your life in jail..."

"It's not me in jail, its Mr. Perfect Andy Pilgrim..."

"I'm your mother and I'm not going to let you get away with this...Just shut up and hold your vicious tongue."

When Sweet Thang put the receiver back in the base, he told Mother Nature what had happened. She looked at him. "You've got to help."

"I know...I'm not going to let anything happen to that good boy."

"Do everything you can...I'm going to keep in touch with Golda to see if there is anything I can do to help calm her down. I know she's out of her mind with fear."

Sweet Thang kissed Mother Nature on the lips, and then started out the door. "That boy is like a son...nothing is going to happen to him, even if it means hurting somebody."

"Be careful baby...don't do anything stupid."

"I won't." He closed the door, walked downstairs and caught a cab. While he waited for the cab, Sweet Thang knew he had to risk his life if that meant saving Andy. He'd let a buddy die in Vietnam and this was his chance to redeem himself. He'd always taken things and now this was a chance to give back. He's always looked after his boy. Andy always gave, gave, and never asked for much in return. Now, Sweet Thang wanted to give. This was his Christian background coming through. The cab pulled in front of the Brownstone.

Upstairs Peter looked at his mother. He knew he had to make a break or he'd be in trouble. He'd though she would come to his defense, but she hadn't. She was more of a good person than he realized.

"I ain't goin' to no jail for anybody."

Suddenly, he leaped forward, pushed his mother down, turned, and sprinted toward the door. "Peter, bring your ass back here." He was in full stride as he bounded down the steps.

He smiled.

When he opened the door, he looked up and there was Sweet Thang. "Where the hell you going?"

Peter was startled.

"Get your wanna-be-thug nigger ass back up them stairs... make a wrong move and I'll make you more of a dead man than Jesse Towns. Try me!"

Peter stepped back into the oncoming palm of Trina. Peter grabbed his face, followed Trina, with Sweet Thang behind him.

"He pushed me down and ran," Trina said. "That sealed your fate."

"I ain't talkin'."

"We'll see about that." Sweet Thang pushed Peter into the apartment.

Marvs, Golda and Sister Love moved toward the door when they heard the noise in the hallway.

"Sweet Thang is that you?" Marvs yelled.

"Yeah... I'll be up in a minute...we have to make a run...calm Golda down. Tell Sister Love to call Mother Nature tell her to get her butt over here pronto. "

"I heard you," Sister Love yelled. "Mother Nature will have your butt for that comment."

"Maybe...Maybe not. It maybe which I've tapped many a time."

"Uh-huh."

"Woman make the call."

"I will."

Marvs walked Golda back into the apartment and Sister

Love followed, headed straight to the telephone.

Sweet Thang closed the door behind him. Peter sat down. He wasn't so confident.

"Now Mr. Peter it's time to talk." Peter looked at Sweet Thang and then he swallowed.

About ten blocks up Gates Avenue, toward Broadway, Andy sat in the 57th Precinct. From his curled up position Andy prayed, "Our father... Who art in heaven... Hallowed be thy name... Thy Kingdom come... Thy will be done on earth as it is in heaven. Give us this day our daily bread... And forgive us our trespasses as we forgive those who trespass against us... Lead us not into temptation, but deliver us from evil... For thine is the kingdom and the power and the glory forever and ever... Amen."

Andy didn't hear the policeman unlock the holding cell. "Following me."

Andy followed the officer from the isolation cell to the holding cell where he saw about twenty other prisoners. There was a small, bulletproof glass window so the prisoners could look out. When the policeman opened the door, the odors from the toilet nauseated him. There were three long benches, no bed and a television hanging from the upper left corner of the cell. The soap opera "As The World Turns" was on the screen.

There were four pay phones. When the policeman closed the door, Andy turned to face the inmates. He backed against the wall and slid down, sitting on the floor where he could see everybody. There was a line waiting, so he waited for an open phone.

Back in Sweet Thang's apartment, the ringing phone startled Mother Nature. She picked up the receiver. "Mother Nature."

"Yes."

"This is Sister Love...your man said to get your ass over here, and now."

"He did!

"Tell that tall lanky idiot, that I'll be there with his surprise."

"I will."

"Thanks for the call."

"Goodbye."

Mother Nature hung up the receiver. She had her signal. Now she must get to Kings County Hospital and find Joshua Bernstein. She was waiting for the call. Now, it was her turn. She knew Bernstein well and he'd come with her to the Brownstone.

Back at Trina's apartment, Peter was defiant. He knew they wouldn't make him talk. "You ain't got nothing on me."

"Oh, well Randall has told the cops that you helped him kill Towns."

"Buddy you're gonna talk."

"Nope."

Sweet Thang smiled.

"All you love is Andy...well he's gonna be a jailbird...just like me."

Trina stood up and walked toward her son.

"I've heard enough venom from you. You're pitiful...you're gonna talk mister and I mean quickly."

Upstairs, the phone rang in the Pilgrims apartment. Golda picked up the receiver.

"Mamma...its Andy."

Golda couldn't believe her ears.

"Mamma."

"Andy...are you okay."

"Yes Ma'am. I'm in a holding cell with other prisoners..."

"Stay calm. We're working to get you out of jail...and soon...Marvs said to trust nobody."

"Mamma, it's gotta be soon...if I don't take that Shakespeare Two final, I can't graduate and then I can't take that job."

"What time is it?"

"It's tomorrow at 10:30...I've got to get off the phone. We

can talk for just one minute. I've got to hang up. I'll call back."

"Andy...Andy...Andy."

Golda hung up the phone and told Marvs and Sister Love what Andy had said about his class.

"He's going to take that test. We're going to get him out of jail and soon."

Out in front of the Kings County Hospital, Sister saw Joshua coming down the steps with his left shoulder in a sling.

"Joshua."

He turned to see Sister Love. "We need your help."

"What."

"They've got Andy in jail...they think he shot you. One of the tenants in the Brownstone told the police that Andy shot you."

"No."

"Andy's in jail."

"Wait...I'm going to talk to my wife."

She watched as he was in a heated discussion with Babbs, telling her he had to go. Then he came back to the cab and got into the backseat with Sister Love. "She's mad."

"Yes...she'll get over it."

The cab sped down Bedford Avenue headed toward Bedford Stuyvesant. Sister Love told Joshua about Andy and how Golda was hysterical and the whole Brownstone was in turmoil.

"We must protect Andy."

"Why are you so interested?"

"He's special... he taught me to trust Black people again. If it wasn't for him, I wouldn't even get in this cab with you. Where is the person who shot me?"

"My man, Sweet Thang, got him at his mother's apartment in the Brownstone. He's waiting for you."

"Good."

At Trina's apartment, Peter was still not talking. "I won't tell you anything..."

"Yes you will."

"You can't make me and you can't prove anything."

"Young boy, I have something that will shock you and make you tell the truth...you're finished."

Peter didn't like the sound of that.

Meanwhile, back at the precinct it was five o' clock and time to feed the incarcerated. The policemen led the prisoners into the next cell where there were two bologna sandwiches and a soda for each prisoner. Andy waited in line for his food. He found a spot to eat his sandwich and drink his soda.

Golda sat by the phone and prayed to Jesus to protect her son and keep him from harm.

"Golda eat something."

"Thank you, but I can't...please Sister Love put those Whitings in the refrigerator and the coconut bread in the bread box...Andy will probably want some..." She stopped in mid-sentence and cried in Marvs arms.

Downstairs, Sweet Thang looked at Peter and smiled.

"What you smiling' for nigger?"

"Your ass in trouble."

"Yeah." Peter laughed. "You're full of shit."

"Stop cursing in front of your mother boy."

"She doesn't love me..."

"Stop your lies...I never stopped loving you. It's because of love that I'm doing what I'm doing tonight. When you walk out of this apartment, I'll have lost a son."

The front doorbell didn't ring much, but the sound surprised Sweet Thang and Trina.

"It's Mother Nature. I knew she'd come through."

"I'll go to the front door." Trina looked at Peter, then walked out of the door. Sweet Thang watched her go down the stairs.

"Prick. You shot that man. You try something and I'll kill your ass now. It's over... You ain't so smart." Sweet Thang laughed out loud. They heard voices in the stairway.

Trina entered first, followed by Mother Nature and then Joshua Bernstein. "Good Afternoon."

Peter slogged back against the chair.

Chapter Fifty-two

The sergeant looked down from behind the counter with the bulletproof glass covering the front counter. He saw two black men and a white man with a sling holding his left shoulder.

"We've come for Andy Pilgrim." Sweet Thang moved closer to the counter.

"Who?" The white sergeant leaned forward.

"Andy Pilgrim... the young man brought in earlier today for the shooting of the fish store owner on Nostrand Avenue."

"Let me check in the back to see what is going on." He turned in his swivel chair and stepped down on the floor behind the counter. He walked back, found a group of policemen and held a ten-minute conversation. Another policeman came toward them. "May I help you?"

"And you are?" Marvs asked.

"I'm sorry, I'm Lt. Newton Skeleton." He extended his hand to Marvs, then Joshua and then Sweet Thang. He smiled when Sweet Thang told him his name. "Please come into my office."

They followed the policeman down a corridor with many large plate glass windows on each side. They walked into the office.

"What seems to be the problem?"

"You've arrested my son Andy Pilgrim for a crime he didn't commit." Marvs didn't blink.

"What!"

"I'm Joshua... the man who was shot." Joshua handed the sergeant some identification. "It was not Andy. He's my friend. It was Peter Paterson. You've got the wrong guy."

"Are you sure?" The sergeant looked at each person as they spoke.

"Yes."

"Andy came into my store to buy his mother, Golda, some Whiting...we talked and he left my business. If you check his pocket, I gave him my card with my home phone number and address. I wouldn't give the man who was about to shoot me my business card?

"Well...Andy left and then this black guy came in, waving a gun. I'd had enough with riots, guns and criminals. I reached for my weapon. I have this permit, so I don't think I did anything wrong." The Sergeant waved his hands in the air. "Before I could get to the gun under the counter, he shot me. It stunned me at first, but then the pain surged throughout my body. I looked right at his face."

"Joshua...were you in the hospital?"

"When I heard that you had Andy here...I couldn't let him stay in that cell. I saw innocent people in Europe jailed and couldn't do anything about it...so here I am...it wasn't Andy."

Marvs couldn't take it anymore. "Sir, how can I get my boy back? He's about to graduate from City College and if he doesn't take his final exam tomorrow, he won't be able to walk down that aisle..."

"Mr. Pilgrim, let me get his paperwork and I'll be back in a few minutes and we'll see what we can do...wait here."

"Always paperwork," Sweet Thang muttered. "Marvs, how can you be so calm?"

"Just be patient...things will work out."

"The only problem now is getting Andy out of jail in time for him to get to City College to take his exam."

Joshua spoke, "Do you think Peter is OK?"

"Yeah, I got him tied up good...he's on the floor and he can't get away...Those two winos will kill him if he tries to get out of that cab."

The lieutenant walked back into the room. "I've got good and bad news...First, the good. If Mr. Bernstein fills out this paperwork and gives a sworn testimony, then we can release your son."

Everybody sighed.

"I'll sign it with pleasure," Joshua said.

"The bad...we can' release him until 9 a.m. tomorrow morning. That's the only time we can finish the legal paperwork. I'll be here myself and I will give him to you at that time. That will give you time to get him to City College...That's the best I can do. He'll have to spend a night in jail."

"Will he be okay?"

"Yes, Mr. Pilgrim, nobody will touch your son."

Marvs put his head on the desk and cried. Joshua and Sweet Thang comforted Marvs. "May I see my boy?"

"Yes. I'll have the sergeant take you to him. Meanwhile, we've got to find Peter Paterson."

"That won't be a problem." The lieutenant turned and looked at Sweet Thang.

"What?"

"We have Mr. Paterson." Sweet Thang laughed.

"Where? How?"

"Just follow me...I'll take you to him. Marvs can visit his boy and Joshua can sign those papers."

The sergeant led Marvs and Joshua to the left, while the lieutenant and two policemen followed Sweet Thang out the door. As he walked across the street to the cab, Sweet Thang waved at the two winos, letting them know they could leave their watch. Nobody touched the cab. He gave each two dollars. They smiled. They could get three bottles of a cheap wine called "Twister." It was only 39 cents a pint.

"I don't believe the guards," Lt. Skeleton said. "Hey, I don't blame you, those winos would kill for that money."

Sweet Thang turned the key and unlocked the back door. There was Peter Paterson lying on the seat with his hands tied. Sweet Thang helped him out of the back. "He won't give much of a fight." Sweet Thang pushed Peter into the waiting arms of two policemen. He closed the cab door.

"Way to give a brotha up to the cops," Peter snarled.

"Right, brotha leech...you won't hurt Andy anymore. If you do, the cops won't get a chance to get you."

"Shut up." One of the policemen yelled at Peter. When they reached the steps to the precinct, Peter wasn't as confident.

"Follow me. I'll lead you to Mr. Bernstein and you can wait for Mr. Pilgrim."

Sweet Thang stepped into the waiting room and saw Joshua.

"Too bad he has to stay even one night in jail." Joshua moved over so Sweet Thang could have a seat.

"I want to say thank you." Sweet Thang extended his hand.

Joshua returned the favor. Meanwhile, Marvs looked through the glass window at Andy. It was the same side of the room from where he had looked at John Randall.

Andy was strong. "I prayed...the Lord is with me and protecting me."

"Good...and we'll have you out of here at nine."

"How's Mamma?"

"She'll be better now that you'll be home in the morning...and we'll have you at City College for that exam.

"Peter?"

"We brought Peter here tonight and he's in jail. Lt. Skeleton said that he won't go near you."

"Andy...remember, we love you. Just believe in yourself and you'll get through this without any scars. Use the power within you that God has given you. Somewhere deep inside, you'll find the strength to get through this night. Draw on your faith in the Lord Jesus Christ. You'll be a stronger person for this and all those other goals will be stepping-stones.

"You're in the lions den like Daniel. Remember, God is with you."

Andy smiled at his father's attempt to encourage him and keep him feeling good about himself.

"Marvs. Thank you for being there for me...I love you."

Andy put his palm on the glass barrier, Marvs did the same and tears came to both of their eyes.

"You're my son and I'll always be there for you."

"I'm the man I am because of you and what you've taught me...always remember that."

The policemen opened the door behind Andy and gestured for him to follow. Andy got up, turned, but then faced Marvs, "I'll be waiting at

nine."

"We'll be on time."

"See you then."

Marvs turned, opened the door and walked down the hallway to where Sweet Thang and Joshua were waiting.

"How'd it go?" Joshua looked concerned.

"Good. Joshua, I want to..."

"Enough already...I've never had so many thank-yous said to me in my life."

Sweet Thang and Marvs laughed. They walked out the precinct door and headed for the cab. They saw the two winos.

"Don't think you two getting any more money!" Sweet Thang roared as he got into the back. Marvs and Joshua got into the front seats. It wouldn't take Marvs long to get Joshua home then get back to his place.

The policemen led Andy back to the original holding cell. He had orders that nobody was to get near this prisoner. He was to be protected. Andy was glad that he was by himself. In a few hours he'd be out of this place and this would seem like a dream, like when they was standing in line at the draft board.

Someone called his name. The voice stunned him. He looked through the bars and recognized the figure as that of John Randall. He was standing at the entrance to his cell, grasping the bars

"Mr. Randall."

"Still the polite young man," Randall smiled. This was one

of the few times that he'd seen the man without a leer.

"Listen...I have only a few minutes. Don't talk. I heard what Peter did to you. When we were planning to kill Towns, all he could talk about was you and how you had everything and he had nothing. He's always been jealous. You don't know it, but I'm one of your guardian angels.

"I've told Mr. Peter that he could talk all he wanted, but he'd better not lay a hand on you. He broke his promise and he'll pay the consequence. That man in Virginia crossed me and died. Towns crossed me and died and now Peter will..."

Andy stared.

"Few people in this world I've ever loved and you and your family have been what I've always wanted. I told your father Marvs how I envy him. Andy, those police couldn't protect you. Now, lay down and get some rest. I'll probably never see you again. Goodbye, and be the man I could never be."

"Mr. Randall...Thank you."

Randall nodded.

"I've never had an uncle or big brother until now."

Andy hadn't noticed, but Lt. Skeleton stood nearby, waiting in the shadows. He stepped out and walked Randall back to his cell.

Andy lay down, closed his eyes and used his palms as a pillow. In the holding cell next to him, Peter Paterson was dead.

Marvs and Sweet Thang walked up the steps to the Brownstone. When they opened the front door, they heard Trina open her door. Marvs smiled and headed up to his apartment.

Sweet Thang lingered and looked at her. "It's done."

"I know...Randall game me a call."

"Did it have to be that way?" Sweet Thang was in shock.

"Peter was a predator. I don't know what happened to my son. I birthed him and brought him into the world. But now the streets got him...I know Peter would've killed me. When he knocked me down, and ran down those steps, I knew something bad was about to happen to him. He'd never been this nervous. Randall told him he'd never let him testify against him. I didn't expect it to come this quick. Randall told me that before he'd let Peter talk, he'd kill or have him killed. I knew when my child went to that jail that he wouldn't come out. I'm tired of talkin', I'm going in here and cry my eyes out."

"Trina." Sweet Thang started toward the door. Trina gently closed the door.

Sweet Thang walked up the steps. He looked back at Trina's apartment. It seemed that the only goodness in the Brownstone came from Sister Love and Golda's apartment. He couldn't believe how Trina seemed so matter-of-fact about the death of her son. Sweet Thang knew from experience that after a while, just living made you numb.

He opened the door and saw Mother Nature, Sister Love, Golda and Marvs sitting on the couch facing the coffee table.

"Where's Trina?" Golda asked.

"She's said she'd talk to everybody later...she wanted to lie down." Sweet Thang lied. But he couldn't continue to lie to his friends. He knew only one way to tell them what had happened at the precinct...

"Peter's dead."

The room was silent.

"What!" Marvs stood up.

"Andy." Golda said.

"He's okay." Sweet Thang sat down next to Mother Nature on the love seat. "He's well protected. Randall will see to that.

"Peter was in big trouble from the moment that he killed Towns.

"Word on the street was that Randall wouldn't let him testify against him. When that lieutenant guaranteed that Andy would be safe, I knew that Peter was in trouble."

"How they kill him?"

"Who knows...stabbed or shot, but since it happened in

prison somebody probably cut his throat."

"I hate to see anybody hurt." Golda moaned. "Poor Trina."

"She'll be okay." Sweet Thang said.

"I think we'd all better get some sleep…we all have had a big day."

"Yeah," Mother Nature added.

"You'll sleep in Andy's bed…what time we get up."

"We'll get up around 7:30 and leave here around 8:30…is that okay?"

"Sure." Sweet Thang headed to Andy's bedroom. Mother Nature followed. Sister Love headed downstairs to her apartment.

Marvs locked the door, headed to his bedroom.

Trina lie in her bed. She looked out the window and wondered where she'd gone wrong. She put a pillow over her face and continued to cry.

At the prison, Andy heard people go in and out of the cell next to him. Then he saw a black shiny plastic bag brought in empty and come out of the cell with a body, covered with a white sheet. Tears rolled down Andy's cheeks. Andy thought about life at the Brownstone and how life before the riots had been calm and peaceful. It seemed that since Towns murder, things had gone wrong. Life was not the same.

Golda thought about her son, but then her thoughts were downstairs with Trina. Her son was coming home from the precinct and Trina's son would never again see the Brownstone. Early morning was going to bring changes in the lives of the people at 423 Gates Avenue.

Marvs was an earlier riser. It wasn't seven, but he had to get up and get everybody else ready for the trip to the police precinct to get Andy.

As Marvs came out of the bathroom, Sweet Thang headed in to get washed up. "You're not a stranger here, get what you need.

"There's fresh washed clothes and towels under the wash basin."

The coffeepot was singing, and pouring out a freshly brewed coffee aroma that circulated throughout the apartment. Marvs smiled. Golda was up and preparing breakfast. She was from the South and if there wasn't a big breakfast of sizzling fat back, which was southern bacon, eggs, grits and homemade biscuits, then breakfast wasn't complete. There weren't going to be any corn flakes in the Pilgrim household this morning.

Andy woke up early from a restless night behind bars. Normally, he'd be headed for the kitchen and on to his Mamma's southern breakfast. He looked up when he heard the jailer unlocked the steel door. He walked over and handed him a small box of corn flakes and a half-pint of milk. There wasn't any sugar. Andy watched the policeman walk out the door and lock it behind him. The sound of the closing door unnerved him.

He poured the milk into the corn flakes and started to eat. He knew when he got home his mother would make up for this breakfast. Andy was alone, but not for long.

After the breakfast, Marvs and Sweet Thang prepared for the trip to the precinct. "I don't want to see my baby in jail. Tell Andy I'll have his favorite dinner of macaroni and cheese, fried chicken and sweet potato pie."

"I'll stay with her for most of the day." Mother Nature gave Sweet Thang a kiss on the cheek.

Marvs and Sweet Thang walked down the stairs and out the door. It was 8:15 am on Gates Avenue and the sun was shining. They arrived at the precinct at 8:30 and walked to the front desk. Lt. Skeleton was waiting for them. "We'll have him here in just a few minutes. We had a terrible accident last night...one of our prisoners died. In fact, it was the one you brought to us."

Marvs and Sweet Thang stared at the lieutenant.

Meanwhile, the sergeant unlocked the door of the cell and told Andy that his father was in the waiting room ready to take him home.

"What you saw last night...Forget." The sergeant led Andy, passed the cells, down the long corridor. He saw Randall, who waved at him. "Remember...you got to make it for us. We sacrificed a lot and don't let it be for nothing. It was either him or you, and as I told you, it wasn't going to be you."

"I won't let you down."

Andy continued to fast-walk down the corridor behind the sergeant. It was 9 am when he walked into the waiting room.

Andy ran and hugged his father and then Sweet Thang.

"We'd better go." Marvs said.

'Thanks you both for everything." Andy had tears in his eyes.

"I brought your books and the things you need for class. Forget this and get your mind on your work. You've got a test to pass."

"Good Luck...sorry for the mistake." Lt. Skeleton opened the door for the threesome as they rushed down the stairs.

"Marvs...get us to the place on time." Sweet Thang jumped into the backseat and Andy in the front. Marvs looked at Andy. "I'm going to get you to the school in plenty of time, then it's up to you to pass that test."

"I will."

Marvs pulled away from the curb, did a U-turn on Gates Avenue and sped down the street. Lt. Skeleton smiled as he saw the cab head toward downtown Brooklyn. All the years of driving a cab, Marvs was going to use that to get his boy to school in time. It was now 9:10 am.

Marvs stayed on Gates Avenue until he found the shortcut through Fort Greene that would take him to Marcy Avenue and The Williamsburg Bridge to Manhattan. Marvs even had Sweet Thang laughing. "You better go boy...I never knew you had it in you to be reckless."

Marvs smiled. "See...you don't know everything about me."

Marvs kept his focus on the traffic. When he got to Marcy

Avenue, he knew he was home free. Marvs weaved between cars. He had thirty minutes when he saw the New York City skyline from the Williamsburg Bridge.

Sweet Thang watched Marvs and couldn't believe his eyes. He was always unruffled, but now he was hyper and determined. Andy looked straight ahead and seemed to be concentrating.

"Andy…Andy, put on the radio. I got to have some music."

Sweet Thang watched as Andy turned the knob and came up on WBLS-AM. The announcer was soothing. "And now we have a song by one of the top soul singer, Mr. Marvin Gaye with "How Sweet It Is.""

The music's beat made Sweet Thang pat his feet, shake his head and bounce around the back seat. "I need the shelter of someone's arms and there you were…"

Marvs talked over the music coming from the radio. "Cut it down a little."

Andy's grin covered his face as he watched his father cross over the Williamsburg Bridge to Delancey Street in Manhattan. Marvs maneuvered through the side streets, all the while working his way uptown. He passed near Central Park, even breaking some traffic laws. When he missed a red light he thought he was in trouble, but the policeman only smiled from his car. Marvs waved. He was in a cab and he was calling in some favors.

When Marvs made it to Central Park West and 96th Street he had twenty minutes to get to City College. The traffic was light and Marvs made every red light. When he got to 125th Street, he made his way over to Convent Avenue. He would make it. Marvs relaxed.

Sweet Thang wanted to say something, but knew better.

When Marvs pulled up on campus, front of Shepherd Hall, Andy jumped out, closed the door. "Thanks…"

"Get in there and pass that test…Your mother will have your favorite dinner when you get home."

Sweet Thang moved from the backseat to the front to sit beside Marvs. "We're proud of you."

Andy grinned. He had about ten minutes to get to his final college exam. A test over Shakespeare's Macbeth. Prof. Tashiro would understand. He looked back and saw Marvs' cab pull away from the curb.

Andy bounded up the steps, pulled the tall wooden door toward him, and stared down the long corridor of the ancient cathedral building. It was the heart of the campus. His exam had been moved from south campus to the main building. The maintenance people were working on the liberal arts building.

He walked down the corridor to room 137, peered into inside and saw Prof. Tashiro. He had five minutes to spare.

"Nice of you to join us...I guess you had nothing better to do. This is probably the most exciting thing happening in your life."

Andy showed Prof. Tashiro and the rest of the class of ten a wry smile. "Nothing ever happens in Brooklyn...just a beautiful quiet and eventless borough." This brought a chuckle from his classmates.

"For all you seniors, this is it...your final exam and then you're off to life in the real world. I know I'm your Shakespeare teacher, but I want to leave you with this thought: always use your imagination and let it help you adjust to life in the future. As a teacher I'm sending you into a world that I will never see. Hopefully, you're prepared to face it. Some of you have faced racial tension and riots, threat of the draft and a possibility of going to the war in Vietnam, a lockout of the College and personal problems. Unlike other graduates, you've faced some of life's problems and have survived.

"Who knows what life will be like in the coming decades of the seventies, eighties or nineties...you've already faced enough to prepare you for the future. Lecture over...best of luck on the exam. For the results, we'll send you a postcard or you can call me at home. Now let's begin."

Prof. Tashiro passed out the infamous blue test booklets students would write in and then the one question exam paper. The gist of it was to describe the theme of Good and Evil in Macbeth. How would you identify this battle in each character? When Prof. Tashiro got to Andy, he smiled. "Good luck...and relax. I hope you do well as a sportswriter in Washington."

"Thanks." Andy placed the exam on his desk. This would be easy.

Meanwhile, Marvs and Sweet Thang headed back to Brooklyn at a less frantic pace.

"He's something special," Sweet Thang observed.

"Yeah...its been tough, but we've almost got him out of college and out of Bedford Stuyvesant. He'll do well in life, but only because he's had an extended family in you, Mother Nature and the rest of the people in the Brownstone to help him through this most difficult part of his life. Thanks for putting your life on the line for Andy."

"He's like the son I never had...nobody, and I mean nobody was going to hurt him in any way. I feel sorry for Peter, but he had chances, and made the wrong choices. I'm into the streets, and that will never change, but to see our youngster doing good...well, he had my support."

"Thanks again...you and Mother Nature are staying for dinner tonight. It's just our way of saying how much we appreciate what you all have done...and don't forget about the block party tomorrow, I'll come and get you."

Sweet Thang nodded his head.

Marvs crossed back over the Williamsburg Bridge and down Marcy Avenue. He was headed for the fresh food open-air markets on Eastern Parkway to get the fresh greens, chicken and other ingredients for the dinner. Marvs and Sweet Thang headed to the A&S department store to see Sister Love. As an employee, she could get jewelry on discount. Golda and Marvs had purchased a 14-karat gold ID bracelet with a Venetian finish on the face, one with Andy's name inscribed in script. This was a graduation present Marvs and Golda had put on layaway six months ago. Sister Love's ten-percent discount made it affordable.

While Andy was in jail, Marvs and Golda had decided to give it to him and make his special dinner. Now, it was not only a graduation present, but also a new lease on life.

Andy finished his exam, talked to some friends, said his good-byes to Prof. Tashiro, walked out of Shepherd, and took the short cut to the subway and his ride to Brooklyn. When he came up the stairs at Fulton and Nostrand Avenue, he looked at the spot on the curb where he'd cried, then continued his walk to Gates. He walked past Gates to the fish market to see if Joshua was in today.

When he walked in the store Joshua came from behind the counter and gave him a one-arm hug.

"Thanks..."

"Don't, Andy... It felt good doing it. When you said you wanted to teach me to trust again...you did. Good luck in DC and be sure to write to me."

"I will." The meeting was brief because Joshua had his wife coming from Queens to pick him up and he didn't want to keep her waiting. "She gets angry."

Andy walked out of the store, feeling good about life. He stopped by the barbershop, got himself a fresh cut and then headed home. When he walked in the door, Golda rushed to hug him, then Mother Nature and finally Sister Love. "We'll eat in about half an hour."

"I want to wash up and rest for a few minutes."

"Good."

Andy walked to his room, stretched across his bed, his long legs hanging over the side. He looked up at the ceiling. This wasn't the hard wood bench that had been his bed last night. This was soft. He sighed because he knew he must do something after dinner. The gentle knock on the door brought him back to reality.

"Andy...it's time for dinner." Andy walked across the

room and kissed his mother on her check. She squeezed his hand.

Marvs smiled from the head of the table, flanked by Mother Nature, Golda's empty chair on the right, Sweet Thang next to Mother Nature, and Sister Love across from him. Andy's spot was at the other end. Everything smelled good and looked even better with the steam from the macaroni and cheese mixed in with the odor of fried chicken and the green beans to make a mouth watering meal.

"We have two surprises for you, one to eat and one...well, we will leave that a surprise." Golda sat down along with Andy. Everybody held hands. It was a good connection.

"Marvs." That meant he was to say grace.

"Gracious Lord we want to thank you for this bountiful meal, and the people around this table. It's been a rough last couple of months here in Brooklyn, but we've made it because of You. When we got down on our knees and prayed, we lay down our burdens, and picked up hope for a new day. Thank you Jesus for this food in your name we pray...and everybody, 'Amen.'"

Everybody talked at once. The people around the Pilgrim's table reacted to the racial riots, Andy being in jail, the block party tomorrow, and the change in attitude for the people of Bedford Stuyvesant.

During the meal, Golda went to the kitchen and brought back her famous Peach Cobbler.

"I can't eat another bite." Sweet Thang grinned, reached, and scooped up two big helpings of cobbler.

"Yeah, can't eat another bite," Mother Nature retorted.

"You ain't come up for air, but once since the food was on the table," Sweet Thang shot back.

Everybody laughed.

Golda and Marvs got up from the table and went into their bedroom and came back with a card and small package wrapped in bright blue paper.

"We wanted to wait until graduation night, but since you

graduated out of jail first, we wanted to have this little party."
Everybody chuckled at Marvs attempt at humor. "Sister Love,
Sweet Thang and Mother Nature helped us get it for you."

Golda handed Andy the card as he stood up. He opened
the card and read the message: "For a unique and wonderful
son. Love Marvs and Mamma." He reached and hugged both
his parents.

Mother Nature and Sister Love cried. Sweet Thang held
Mother Nature's hand, while she reached for Sister Love.
When Andy finished embracing his parents, Golda gave him
the package. Andy tore the paper off the package and opened
the jewelry box. The gold sparkled in the light. The ID bracelet
was perfect. Andy handed the box to his parents and Marvs
and Golda put it on his wrist. He kissed his mother on her
cheek, embraced Marvs and then walked around the table
kissing Mother Nature and Sister Love.

"A hug please," Sweet said.

"I wasn't going to kiss you anyway." Andy embraced the
man who had done do much for him since he came to Gates
Avenue.

Tears formed in Andy eyes as he looked at the people and
felt the love coming from around that table.

"Thank you for being here for me...Sweet Thang when I
needed you, you didn't let me down...Mother Nature has
shown me ways of tackling life's many difficult
situations...Sister Love has taught me not to be so serious, but
to see life with a smile on my face...Marvs has shown me how
to be a man...Mamma's unconditional love has given me the
courage to tackle anything that has come into my life...Thank
you and I hope to give back what you have given me."

Everybody walked into the living room and sat down. It
was the season for love in the Brownstone.

Chapter Fifty-three

Marvs walked in the fourth-floor apartment after taking Mother Nature and Sweet Thang home, while Sister Love went downstairs to put Mr. Raymonds to bed.

"You know how old men are." Sister Love laughed walking past Marvs.

Andy was on the phone when his father came into the apartment.

He ran back into the room with a smile that could light up a marquee on a Broadway Theater. "I passed Tashiro's exam with a ninety-one. I will graduate."

Everybody hugged again. "Thank you Jesus." Golda looked up to the heavens. "My boy is a college graduate..."

"And my boy." Marvs smiled.

"Thanks for everything...make sure you call everybody."

"We will." Golda headed for the phone.

Everybody was settling down. "I'm going to run to the candy store for a second." Andy kissed his mother on her cheek. "I'll be back in a few minutes."

"Andy...be careful."

"I will Mamma." Andy fingered the gold bracelet and closed the door behind him. He wanted to run to the store and get cards to send to everybody over the next few weeks.

Andy walked past the barbershop and caught Mr. Possum, just as he was about to close the door. "Andy."

"Need some thank you cards."

"Get 'em quick."

Andy rushed to the shelf in the back, grabbed the box of cards, and walked to the counter to pay for his purchase. "Finishing school soon...I'll graduate in about four weeks."

"Good luck."

"Thanks." Andy paid Mr. Possum and walked back toward the Brownstone. He crossed the street so he could see the Brownstone. All the lights were on in the building. He thought about the different lives. Andy walked across the street, ran up the steps, opened the door and walked back into his world.

Andy went down to the basement. The door was unlocked. It was dark and he wanted to see this place and reflect on all the events. The murder, the plotting to destroy this building. People had died. It was a waste.

He walked out the door, bounded up the stairs and knocked on Trina's door. He waited for her to answer.

"Yes."

"It's me, Andy."

The door opened slowly. Trina's eyes were red from crying, but she forced a smile.

"How you doing? ...I'm so happy that you are well."

"Thanks...I came see you and tell you how sorry I am about what happened to Peter..."

"Don't feel bad...I'll grieve enough for the both of us. Andy, he had choices and he didn't make the right ones. When I found out he killed Towns, I should have gone to the police. I hoped he'd change, but he didn't and I wasn't going to let him kill another person.

"Sometimes, you have to make decisions and this one cost him his life. There will always be hurt inside, but I'll manage. My other children must see a different life. We'll move from this Brownstone and find someplace else. I'm thinking about moving back down to Virginia. They say things are changing."

Andy reached out and touched her hand.

Trina smiled. "Keep going in the right direction and don't let anybody hold you back. Like old Satchel Page said, 'Don't look back because something is gaining on you.' I still love you Andy. Now, get out of here and don't let the past keep you from your goals."

"I won't." Andy gave her a kiss on the cheek.

Trina closed the door behind him. She rested her head on

the door.

Andy continued up the stairs, passed his own apartment and up to the roof. This was his last stop before going back to Marvs and Golda. He had to do this, get the fear out of him. He must learn to face fear, not to cower.

As he turned the knob, opened the door, and waked on to the roof of the Brownstone, Andy was apprehensive. His steps were tentative, but he put one foot in front of the other and walked around. There weren't any whistling sounds or bullets flying, just the noises coming from the street, and the occasional jet engine roaring as the planes roared overhead in route to LaGuardia or Kennedy airports.

Andy listened intently a particular sound. It was low, but when the wind changed directions, the sound was louder. It was music. Somebody had the radio station WBLS on and the songs were coming through louder.

It was The Drifters song "Up On The Roof." For the first time in a long while he felt unconfined as he started to sway to the music. Andy could dance, he just usually didn't. Now, he didn't care who saw him. Andy danced with the music and sang the lyrics:

"When this old world starts getting me down and people are just too much for me to face…I climb way up to the top of the stairs and all my cares just drift into space. On the roof… The only place I know…where you just have to wish to make it so. I get away from the hustling crowd and all that rat race noise in the streets…"

Andy was really into singing the song as he swirled, jumped up into the air, moved his head with the music and let out all the frustrations, uptightness, and anxiety that was pressing him down. He continued to sing, "Up on the roof… When I came feeling tired and weak, I go up where the air is fresh and sweet… Up On The Roof…Let's go up on the roof." As the song ended, so did Andy's dance routine. He thought about what the people that knew him would have thought.

He was sweaty, but his exhilaration prevented him from

feeling tired. He sat down on the roof as the announcer played song after soulful song. Andy jumped to his feet, put his arms out wide, twirled and spun around, creating a dizzy feeling. He headed to the stairs.

Andy closed the door to the roof and, locking it from the inside, walked down the one flight to his parent's apartment. He knocked on the door. Golda smiled as she opened the door.

"We've been waiting." Golda kissed Andy on the cheek.

Marvs was on the couch, ready to watch the eleven o'clock news. He looked up and winked. "I didn't know you could dance like that."

"No way...you two didn't watch me..."

"After what happened, we weren't going to take any chances."

Andy smiled. "I have a lot of talent in a lot of areas." Andy knew he had a future.

He sat down on the couch as Golda went into the kitchen to finish cooking the rest of the food that she was bringing to the block party.

All was quiet at the Pilgrim's.

Chapter Fifty-four

The B-52 bus route was changed so the residents of the four hundred block could have this unity party. This party had been planned for weeks. It was a chance to help the businesses which had been damaged or destroyed during the Bedford-Stuyvesant racial riots.

The sunlight made everything bright and the multi-culture atmosphere reflected the change in the neighborhood. There were samples of food from Barbados, Jamaica, other West Indian islands, southeast Asia and the southern United States. The block had many new people, and now this was a chance to unify the community.

The food booths were at each end of the block with the middle open for games, dancing area and a big music system in the center. It was quiet for most of the time until the Deejay put on Jackie Wilson's hit song. The trumpets and drums opened with Wilson's high pitch voice setting the mood: "Your love's lifting me higher...than I've ever been lifted before...Your love's lifting me higher and higher..."

The dancing area was filling up with people from the neighborhood. Everybody stopped when Sister Love and Mr. Raymond stole the show. Sister Love was moving with the music and Mr. Raymond was doing his own thing. Nobody could figure out what. People were laughing, hooting, and slapping five with each other.

Golda, Marvs, Mother Nature and Sweet Thang were sitting on the steps of the Brownstone watching the spectacle.

"What the hell he doin'," Sweet Thang observed.

"I tell you what, old as he is, somebody better alert the emergency room at Kings County that they'll have a victim," Mother Nature answered.

"I knew Sister Love was crazy, but I thought Mr. Raymond had better sense," Marvs said.

"Not really." Golda grinned.

"Did Andy get here yet?" Marvs asked.

"Not yet," Golda said.

"He's bring Leslie here for a while," Mother Nature said.

"I like her, but sometimes I wonder if this is the right move for him with Leslie," Golda wondered out loud. She hoped that Leslie was right for Andy. Golda promised Marvs that this was one decision that Andy had to make on his own without help from his parents.

Golda had had second thoughts after she'd met Leslie's parents. They were light-skinned professional Blacks who tended to look down on Blacks with darker skin. They seem to tolerate whoever was more of a pecan color and had curly hair. When they saw Marvs, who was dark, they gave him that once over. The smile from Leslie's parents was phony. Golda was reddish in tone and they felt comfortable with her.

Golda hoped that Andy would see through this and find him somebody that he could respect, communicate with and have an honest relationship. She promised not to be an interfering mother.

"Golda, be nice when Leslie gets here," Marvs cautioned. "Although her parent don't like dark-skinned Blacks, Leslie doesn't seem to mind. Andy is dealing with the daughter not the mother."

Golda gave a knowing look to Mother Nature."

"These people kill me being color struck," Mother Nature said. "Yeah, what that saying 'Blacker the berry the sweeter the juice'...well, I can't stand uppity niggers."

"Sweet Thang help me."

Sweet Thang smiled, then looked away. He almost broke his neck laughing when he saw Sister Love helping Mr. Raymond up the stairs to a seat on the stoop in front of Sweet Thang.

Everybody laughed.

"Good for your old ass." Mother Nature wasn't bashful. "Sister Love, why you trying to kill that old man?"

Sweet Thang was doubled over on his side laughing.

Marvs had his head in Golda's lap.

Sister Love put her hands on her hips. "Trying to kill him, you gotta be kiddin'. This old man doesn't have enough insurance to bury him in a wood box. Besides, everyday he takes a chance when walks down the block. When Mr. Raymond goes to get the *New York Daily News* in the morning, I have to watch to make sure that the undertakers from the two funeral homes don't snatch him."

Sweet Thang was howling.

People from the streets looked up at Sweet Thang jumping up and down and Marvs leaning over the side of the stoop.

"You two stop embarrassing everybody," Golda said, laughing.

Mother Nature jumped up and joined Sweet Thang.

Mr. Raymond was too tired and sore to reply.

"Sister Love stop it. Quit making fun of such a nice man as Mr. Raymond," Golda admonished.

"He's got you folks fooled. He's a cranky old fool, especially when he can't play his numbers or get his daily shot of vodka." Sister Love was in rare form.

A crowd gathered in front of the Brownstone.

Andy and Leslie, holding hands, saw the crowd from the corner.

"What's going on?" Leslie carried a bag from Keys jewelry store on Broadway.

Andy laughed.

"What's all those people doing in front of our building?"

Andy saw Sister Love with her hands on her hips at the top of the steps. He knew that she was having fun at Mr. Raymond's expense. When they got to the back of the crowd things were winding down and the crowd was going back to the dance area.

Andy and Leslie made their way up the steps.

"How's everybody?" Andy asked.

"Great." Sweet Thang smirked.

"All except Mr. Raymond, who looks kind of under the weather." Mother Nature couldn't help but laugh.

"Everybody is okay. Congratulations on that exam grade," Sister Love said. "Come here and give me a hug. Your girlfriend won't mind." Andy walked up the final two steps and also gave Mother Nature and his mother hugs. Then he shook hands with Sweet Thang and Marvs.

Everybody admired his bracelet and talked about the graduation in about four weeks. "I'm going to leave my diploma here and put it up with the one from Bushwick High."

Andy then gave each person on the steps a card. "Thanks for helping make all this possible." And then he went into the bag and picked out five small packages. "You know when I worked last summer, well, I was doing it for a reason." Andy gave each person a small package.

"I want you to look at them when we leave and please give this one to Trina. Mamma I'll be back early, because I have to go up to City College tomorrow to sign some final papers." He kissed his mother again on the cheek.

Sweet Thang opened his package and it was a gold bracelet. Marvs had a gold ID bracelet in his package inscribed "Love, your son Andy." Sister Love and Mother Nature had gold chains in their boxes. Golda had a gold chain with three small replicas of baby shoes. In top part of each shoe were birthstones for Marvs, Golda and Andy.

Mr. Raymonds watched and laughed. "I helped the boy find the right place to go to, he wanted to give me something, but I told him 'No' because him making something of himself was the best gift to give an old man."

Sister Love reached down and kissed Mr. Raymond on the forehead.

Golda walked toward the door. She saw the party going strong and moved inside. She turned. "I'll be right back."

She knocked on Trina's door. Trina opened the door. Golda handed her the package.

"Andy worked last summer and bought these tokens of his appreciation for us. He wanted to thank everybody in the building for their help.

"Trina, only another mother could understand the depth of emotion that you're feeling now. I do."

Trina hugged Golda. "Thank you." She closed the door behind her.

Trina walked to her recliner and opened the card. 'Dear Mrs. Paterson, I want to thank you for all you have done for me over the years. This will not replace Peter, but I wanted you to have this. Love, Andy.'

She put the card down and opened the package. It was a gold necklace. She rubbed it and then put it around her neck. She held the card against her chest and cried.

Golda and the rest of the people were now in the streets enjoying the party and the unity. It was a happy day for the residents of the Brownstone and the people of Gates Avenue.

Andy took Leslie home. Outside Leslie's front doors, Andy was saying his goodbyes.

"I'm glad you decided to go to Howard University in the fall. We'll be separated for only a few months until then. I'll be traveling between Brooklyn and Washington a lot in the summer."

Andy pulled Leslie close to him.

They kissed.

Chapter Fifty-five

Andy couldn't sleep the night before his graduation. It reminded him of the night before he was to face the draft board. The day went slow, in fact the month prior to this day, went quickly for the Pilgrims as they prepared for Andy's graduation and his leaving for Washington. It was an emotional rollercoaster.

The house was frantic.

Andy's cap and gown were on his bed and his room was in disarray. He was dressed when his mother walked into his room. They had two hours to get to the commencement ceremonies.

"Andy." Golda smiled. "How do I look?"

"Great." Andy kissed his mother.

Marvs walked through the door. "You look great son. I got the cab. Sweet Thang rented a car so he could bring Sister Love, Mr. Raymonds and Mother Nature. Trina will ride with us. Everybody ready?"

"How's Leslie getting there?" Golda asked.

"Her parents," Andy said.

Andy reached for his cap and gown that would go over his black suit. Marvs was the last one out of the apartment door and made sure everything was locked. As they walked down the stairs, Sister Love, Mr. Raymonds and Trina followed them. Everybody dressed well for this special night in Manhattan.

Sweet Thang and Mother Nature were waiting for Sister Love and Mr. Raymonds to get in the backseat. Marvs, Goldie, Andy and Trina got in the cab. It was a tight fit.

The ride wasn't long, because the rush hour was over. When the parties drove onto 34th Street, everybody felt a twinge of excitement. It was a special night!

The Felt Forum at the Madison Square Garden Center at

34th and Eighth Avenues was the scene of The City College's One-Hundred and Twenty-Third Commencement. It was a time of graduation for over 3,000 seniors.

The arena was filling up and Andy looked around to see where his parents were sitting so he could wave to them when the seniors receiving a Bachelor of Arts degree were asked to rise from their seats and move their tassels from the left of the cap to the right side to signify graduation. Before Andy could get in his graduation line Marvs met him in the corridor.

"Andy, let's change shoes. We wear the same size. My shoes are newer and I want you to look the best."

When both men changed shoes, a moment that would bond them forever. Marvs had sacrificed so much for Andy and he was still providing for his son. Andy didn't say a word, but reached and gave his father a man-sized bear hug.

Marvs went back to his seat and Andy went into the back of the Felt Forum to join the other CCNY graduates. The graduation music signaled the senior's procession to enter the arena. When all the graduates were seated, the order of exercises began.

There was the invocation, and address by City College president Jasper Cooper, a presentation to the college from the graduating class and then the conferring of degrees. The deans of the five schools presented the candidates for the academic degrees. When it came time for the College of Liberal Arts and Science, it was Andy's turn to stand up.

The graduates stood up and emotion surged through Andy's body. He looked up and saw his family and all the people from the Brownstone. His eyes went from Marvs, Golda, Mother Nature, Sweet Thang, Trina, Sister Love, Mr. Raymonds and Leslie.

When the dean said, "You are now graduates!", in unison the seniors switched the tassels from one side to the other to become graduates of The City College of New York.

Andy saw his mother crying in Marvs' arms, Mother Nature in Sweet Thang's arms and Sister Love in Mr.

Raymond's.

At that moment he wanted to be in the balcony with Leslie.

The recessional was quick and he found the table with his name. He signed for his diploma and made his way to where his family would meet. They were all in a group.

When he came up, they all tried to grab him at once, but his mother got their first. He handed her his diploma, "Mamma, it's been a long time coming."

"I know baby. It's worth it. My baby is a college graduate."

Everybody clapped.

Andy hugged every person that came to see him graduate. Everybody was going to their cars for the ride back to Brooklyn and the graduation party in Sister Love's apartment in the Brownstone.

Andy walked out of the Felt Forum into the cool New York City evening with his mother and Leslie on either side. Sweet Thang's party was the first to leave, followed by Leslie's family. It would be interesting to see how Leslie's parents reacted to the people in the Brownstone. Marvs, Golda, Andy and Trina walked to the yellow cab.

Chapter Fifty-six

The month between Andy's graduation from City College and his departure for Washington D.C. was a period of time where he didn't want to become a piece of driftwood in the river of life. He wanted direction and to take control of the events that would form his existence.

During this time span, Andy's life in Brooklyn was the same as it had always been. His daily routines were the same. The only difference was that he was preparing for his departure to Washington. The Pilgrims spent a weekend in D.C. preparing Andy's apartment. They rented a van and carried all his personal items to his apartment near the offices of *The Washington Star*. His parents met the editors of the paper and saw where he would spend his first years as a reporter.

Everything was ready for him to start his new life.

The last week in the Brownstone in Brooklyn was filled with good-byes and tears. He had two days remaining before Marvs would take him to Penn Station for the train that would take him to Washington.

Joshua wasn't in the fish market, but Andy didn't want to leave Brooklyn without saying goodbye. The phone rang and Joshua was cheerful. "Good Afternoon, Joshua Bernstein speaking."

"Joshua, this is Andy."

"How you doing Mr. Pilgrim?"

"Good, I want to thank you for all you have done for me."

"Stop, I know how you feel. I saw your face. I did it from the heart. You have a great future,don't look back. Go out and help people and make sure to send me some of the articles you write."

"I will, but I want to say thank you."

"Remember, you old friend Joshua will be here for you.

Call if you need anything."

"Joshua, you will always be my friend."

"That means a lot to me Mr. Pilgrim, good luck and take care."

Andy spent the rest of the day visiting friends and then going around Brooklyn running errands with Golda and Marvs. They paid bills, bought a few clothes and then some Chinese dinner. His parents pulled up in front of Leslie's house.

"I won't be here too long, just want to say goodbye to Leslie. I have to get up early so Marvs can get me to Penn Station."

Andy leaned over and kissed his mother's cheek and patted Marvs on the shoulder. He closed the cab door, waved, and walked up the brick walkway to Leslie's house.

As Marvs pulled away from the curb, Andy was knocking on the front door. Leslie answered with a smile that warmed his heart.

"Hi baby." Andy embraced Leslie and the kiss, between the two young lovers, was a unifying force. They held each other tight. They finally separated and smiled at each other.

"I hate to see you go to D.C."

"I know." Andy held her tight for a few moments, then they walked from the front door to the living room, sat down next to each other on the couch. The radio was tuned to the soul station WBLS which was playing some mellow rhythm and blues songs. The Delfonics' "La La Means I Love You" was part of the atmosphere in Leslie's apartment.

Andy and Leslie held hands and listened to the lyrics and let their dreams unite.

They kissed.

They talked.

They discussed the future. "I sent my application to Howard University. I'll be there in September, so we can be near each other."

"That means we'll be separated only a few weeks."

Andy smiled at Leslie, leaned over and kissed her lips.

It was getting late and Andy knew if he didn't leave now, he wouldn't. "Got to go."

"I know." Leslie hugged and kissed Andy. They parted, got up from the couch and walked hand-in–hand to the front door. They hugged again, then Andy opened the door.

Their lips touched for a few seconds and then they separated. The kiss was good.

"I'd better go." Andy pulled away from Leslie, stepped out the door and smiled.

"Andy."

He turned to face Leslie.

"Love you."

"Love you back." Andy smiled, kept walking and jogged around the corner to catch the B-52 bus that was turning from Broadway onto Gates Avenue.

The bus ride was about fifteen minutes to 423 Gates Avenue. and when Andy walked into the door of his parents' apartment, Golda and Marvs were asleep. He closed the door, locked it, and then went into his bedroom.

Golda raised up from the bed, smiled, then laid her head back on the pillow and breathed a sigh of relief.

She fell asleep.

Chapter Fifty-seven

The morning dawned bright on Gates Avenue as the sunlight filtered through the half-closed blinds that covered Andy's window.

This was his last day in Brooklyn.

Andy heard his mother stirring in the kitchen, smelled the sizzling bacon and the brewing coffee. He walked to the bathroom. "Andy!"

"I'm up Mamma."

"Breakfast ready in a few minutes. Marvs getting dressed. He packed the car earlier. I'll have breakfast in a few minutes."

Andy put on a pair of faded blue jeans, white t-shirt with the purple letters "CCNY" inscribed across the front. He put on a pair of sweat socks and the new sneakers that his parents had bought him. The last thing he put on was the gold bracelet that Marvs and Golda gave him.

Andy walked into the kitchen, saw his parents already seated at the table. Andy sat down and Marvs blessed the table with an emotional prayer. The Pilgrim family held hands.

"I'll miss you baby."

"Mamma, don't cry. I'll be home every other weekend. You and Marvs must come and stay with me any time you want to visit."

"We will," Golda said.

Marvs smiled.

Breakfast was quick.

Andy's train was leaving at 11:30 a.m. and Marvs had two hours to get him to the station on time.

"We don't have to set any speed records today." Marvs smiled.

"Yeah, that was fun. Riding through Manhattan to get me

to City College for that final exam. We got to do it again."

"I don't' thinks so." Marvs headed to the bathroom.

Andy looked at his mother. She paused. "Baby, I'm so proud. I'll be strong and not cry. I can't see you get on that train. I'm going to stay here, so you call me when you get to D.C."

"I will."

Andy and Golda embraced.

Golda thought about how it seemed like yesterday when he was a wide-eyed little kid. Now he was leaving her. She held him tight.

Marvs came out of the bathroom, kissed Golda, opened the apartment door and walked down the staircase. He didn't want to leave the car unattended any longer.

Andy kissed his mother and followed his father down the stairs. Golda closed the door behind him, leaned her head on the door and cried.

As Andy was walking down the stairs, Sister Love opened her door, came out and hugged him. Then came Mother Nature and Sweet Thang, who had spent the night in the Brownstone.

There weren't any words exchanged, only hugs and tears.

Andy looked over his shoulder, waved and kept walking. Trina came out and embraced Andy. She quickly turned, crying, and ran back into her apartment. Andy kept walking down the stairs. He looked down one last time at the stairs leading into the basement, which caused a chill to attack his body. Andy kept walking toward the front door. He bounded down the outside steps, then looked back at the windows in the Brownstone.

Andy's eyes scanned the front of the Brownstone, moving from apartment to apartment. Trina waved, then as he gazed upward he saw Sister Love and Mother Nature embracing and waving at him. Finally, he focused on his mother. Golda had both palms on the window, then she waved.

Andy waved to his mother and all the people, then he

turned, headed toward the yellow cab, and left behind him the Brownstone in Brooklyn.

Made in the USA
Columbia, SC
27 June 2020